Prologue

His Majesty, Lord Robert Bruce, King of the around his aged frame. As rain pelted the sides of the castle at Edinburgh, he felt like he could detect the dank air seeping into his bones. Indeed, he felt that he was not long for this world. The year was 1329 and he had just made official the paperwork making his son David the official heir, and his grandson Robert Stewart the official regent. There were just a few more orders of business that had to be taken care of before he left for Cardross, where a doctor had supposedly conjured some miracle cure for his ails.

A knock sounded at the door and Robert conjured a "Come," from somewhere deep in his chest.

The door opened and in stalked two powerful examples of Scottish heritage.

Lord Alexander Sinclair, Duke of Roslin, was a large, sturdily-built man with large hands and a full head of deep red hair that had turned a stark white at his temples. His build and the still-handsome features of his face belied his 59 years, making most consider him to be a much-younger man. Beside him stood his eldest son William, a portrait of his father at a younger age. The two men strode forward and kneeled before their king.

"Stand," he told them softly. It had become harder over the passing months to raise his voice in the strength he was used to. They followed his command nonetheless.

"We report at your command, Majesty," said the elder Sinclair.

"Cut the shit, Alex. We have known each other far too long for that."

Sinclair chuckled. "That we have, Robert."

The two old comrades exchanged a meaningful look. "I see your boy has come to look even more like you."

A hand of fatherly affection fell on William's shoulder. "He is far more handsome than I," he laughed, "at least according to his mother and his wife."

Robert's chuckle was stronger than before, though he sent a mock-severe look at the young man. "Seventeen years and already married?" He shook his head.

William looked properly self-conscious. "We are in love, Majesty."

Robert laughed out loud. "Is that what they call it now?"

All three men shared in his humor. When the King looked up, his visage was serious. "Have you thought about my offer?"

Again, Alexander looked at his son. "I have, Majesty. And it was unnecessary. The Order will be pleased to accept your grandson. And I will be happy to see my son a member as well, after the proper forms have been observed."

A look of confusion shone on William's face. "What are you talking about, Father?" His soft voice did not reflect the strength that both older men knew the youth had.

King Robert pushed himself up from his throne and lifted a sword that had leaned against it. "Kneel, William."

William did so. Robert touched his left shoulder with the flat of the blade. "In the name of God, St. Michael, and St. Andrew, I dub thee a Knight." He reversed the blade and extended the hilt of the sword with a practiced flourish. "Rise, Sir William Sinclair."

William reached out and took the hilt, rising to his feet. Robert looked over at the elder Sinclair, noticing the glint of pride in his eyes. He turned back to Sir William Sinclair. "Excuse us please, Sir William. Pietro will afford you with a room for tonight. I will see you in the morning for breakfast."

William bowed his head to his king, then his father before leaving. Robert dropped back into his throne with a heavy sigh. He looked up at Alexander, calculating.

"So, Grand Master, several of our fellows are here. Can we convene tomorrow after we have shared supper?"

The Master of the Temple chuckled, scratching at the stubble on his face. "I believe we can accommodate you, Majesty."

A one-eyed man-at-arms led Sir William Sinclair and Sir Robert Stewart into the bowels of the castle. It was rumored that a huge basement had been excavated here when the structure was built, but by royal decree, none were allowed to venture into it without the express permission of the King of Scotland.

Sir Robert was a tall, skinny man with a thin face and thinning hair. Indeed, many who saw both of them would doubt they were related. But William's mother was cousin to Robert's sister, and William had grown up in the circles populated by men like Sir Robert and the King. In fact, his mind still reeled a bit at the honor done him by His Majesty the evening before. His father had refused to discuss anything further when he returned to their chambers and in the afternoon had ordered him to pray and prepare himself, still unwilling to discuss what was to come after the sky was thrown into darkness.

The man-at-arms stopped before a knight clad in strange white robes. A white cape covered his shoulders while his blade was large and held by a belt threaded with silver. The man-at-arms bowed deeply. "Brother Knight, I have returned with those the Worshipful Master called for."

The knight nodded. "Very well, Brother Sergeant. I will have him informed directly. You are dismissed."

The man-at-arms placed his right hand over his heart and bowed again. With no further word, he turned on his heel and returned up the stairs. William looked around the room. It was not large and with three men in it, seemed crowded. There was a large oak door set in two different walls. The third wall also had a door, this one open and showing the stairs up which the man-at-arms had retreated. The fourth wall was blank and held a torch in a brace.

William's attention returned to the white-robed knight who knocked three times on the oak door. After a moment, his knocks were returned from within and the door opened. A whispered conversation was held, followed by the door closing again. When it did, he turned back around and rested his back against the wall alongside that door.

Minutes passed in silence before the other door opened. William was taken aback at the appearance there of Sir Kenneth Taggart, the Duke of Elderslie. Sir Kenneth had spent much time in the Sinclair household over the years and a few years before had taken a wife from Roslin, one of the daughters of a minor nobleman from William's father's lands. It was said that Sir Kenneth and Sir Alexander had been longtime friends and had fought the English alongside King Robert himself. He was dressed like the guard outside the door, but his belt was threaded with gold and the sheath holding his sword was of matching metal.

Sir Kenneth looked over both of the younger men. "Sir Robert, come with me."

Robert nodded and followed him back into the dark room. The knight waiting outside with

The minutes passed in interminable silence and William could not help but wonder what was to happen next.

After an endless space of time, the door opened again. Kenneth again stepped forward. "Sir William," he said.

William stepped forward. The door was closed behind him and it took a moment for his eyes to adjust to the darker room. "Strip off your clothes and put this on."

Kenneth extended his arm, holding a plain white robe. William did as instructed. When the robe was on him, Kenneth stepped behind him. A blindfold covered his eyes. Kenneth lead him forward a few steps and pressed his hand into a fist. The older knight lifted his arm and extended it forward. He made William knock three times on an oak door.

Within a minute, his knocks were echoed back and the door opened.

A familiar voice, that of Lord Malcolm Davidson, came to William's ears. "Who comes here?" the voice demanded out of the darkness.

Chapter 1

Roslin, Scotland, 1283

The sunlight filtered through the trees as young Alexander moved quietly through the trees. He had often moved so, armed only with stones, in search of rabbits and squirrels. But today, he was unarmed and in search of finer prey.

Fiona was five years older than the lad's twelve. And she was utterly beautiful, with hair the rich dark red of a dying fire and laughing blue eyes that reflected the color of the loch on a brilliant summer day.

Alexander had watched as she and her two sisters had gathered their things and lit off on the path to a secluded section of the loch for a mid-afternoon swim.

Now the boy dropped to a crouch on a flat place near the water and parted the branches with his hand.

The first thing he saw was Fiona's sister Anna. He knew she was five years older than Fiona and married with two sons. She stood naked in the sunlight, releasing her brown hair from its bun to flow to her round bottom. She was plump and Alexander was captivated by the sight of her full sloping breasts. His eyes dropped to the thick mass of brown curls below her round belly and he was aware of the heat radiating from between his own legs.

His face heated as he reached down to touch his erection through his kilt. His eyes were drawn next to the form of Brigid, Fiona's twin sister. She was thin with light red hair. She laughed at something Anna said and swam deep underwater toward her older sister, who has waded out from the shore.

Alexander experienced a thrill as Brigid swam around Anna and swatted her plump bottom. Fiona ran out of the woods and leaped into the water, splashing her sisters.

The boy admired her naked form when she surfaced and began to lift his kilt, intent on pleasuring himself.

A strong hand clamped over his mouth and a stronger arm gripped him around the chest. Alexander put up his mightiest struggle, but to no avail. A small part of Alexander's mind noted calmly that, despite his struggles, the man who held him made no noise as he moved through the forest.

They broke out into a clearing where the road ran. Alexander was roughly tossed to the ground. He looked around quickly, taking stock of his situation.

A woman, a beautiful woman, stood beside a carriage on the road. A footman with a scar down his cheek glared dangerously, his hand moving in a flash to the hilt of his knife, which was halfway out when he recognized Alexander's captor.

Alexander looked up at the man who had thrown him to the ground. He was gargantuan with muscle. His thick, black, curly hair hung to his collar and framed a face of granite-like strength. He wore pants rather than the kilts Alexander was used to seeing.

A soft, Irish-accented voice interrupted Alexander's increasingly-frightened examination. "Who is this brigand, husband?"

The man's features softened as he turned his face to answer his wife. "He was spying on some girls at a nearby lake."

He woman chuckled lightly. "Were they pretty, my love?" She climbed into the carriage as his face reddened. Then he looked at Alexander.

"Come on, boy." Alexander slowly got to his feet.

The big Irishman lifted the boy to the seat next to the footman, then mounted a horse that Alexander had not noticed before.

It was a magnificent roan stallion, its coat shining in the sun that filtered through the trees. He looked up at the footman and grinned. "We will take the lad before Sir Edward."

Alexander's eyes got big at the sound of his father's name. The Irishman laughed as he rode ahead.

At that particular moment, however, Sir Edward St. Clair's thoughts were far from the activities of his son. Rather, they were entirely directed toward the boy's mother.

He had been discussing the weather outlook with one of the nearby farmers when his wife had sauntered by, a sparkle flashing in her eye.

Edward had gotten the message and politely excused himself, trailing Irina through the halls to their private chambers. It was at the door to those chambers that he had been intercepted by his seneschal Philip, who had himself been detained by the abbot telling him that young Alexander had skipped his lessons that morning. Edward had rushed his administrative chief away, promising he would speak with the boy.

He stepped through the sitting room in his chambers into the bedroom, and was greeted by the sight of his wife's naked backside. He closed the door between the rooms as she slyly smiled back at him over her shoulder.

Edward crossed the room in three long strides and caught her up in his arms, his hands squeezing her full breasts. She pressed her bottom against the stiffness under his kilt and moaned her pleasure as his fingers rolled and squeezed her nipples. His lips and teeth nibbled at her neck. She closed her eyes as one hand brushed over her stomach to her pubic hair. His fingers found her moist opening and fondled the stiff nub there. Her hands clutched at his kilt, pulling it up until she could feel his hot flesh throbbing against her.

She took it as long as she could, then turned to face him. He started to disrobe and she wrapped her fingers around his engorged member, stopping him from undressing. "No," she said. "Right now." She laid back on the bed and he followed, mounting her and driving himself into her damp channel.

Irina moaned loudly as he pushed himself in with stroke after deep stroke. Her ankles crossed behind his back and lifted her to meet each rhythmic thrust. Her hands grasped at his back, pulling his shirt up and bunching it in her grip. She could feel him swell and knew he was close. She smiled at the knowledge that her own pleasure was rapidly approaching as well. Her eyes closed and she was lost.

With a scream of utter pleasure, she was swept onto the shores of orgasm. A small part of her senses felt the small explosions of extra joy that came as her husband expended his seed into her womb.

She wrapped her arms around her strong husband's back and whispered in his ear, "I love you."

Edward breathed hard into her hair and pushed himself up to look into her light-blue eyes. "And I you, wife."

Irina smiled as they kissed.

Unfortunately, Edward St. Clair, the Earl of Roslin, could not spend the rest of the day in bed with his younger, energetic wife.

As she continued to lay there, he rose and crossed the room to wash himself in the basin. When he was clean, he busied himself putting his clothes to rights. It was then that he noticed that his shirt had been ripped in the back by his wife in the depths of her pleasure.

He wheeled around and addressed her with mock annoyance. "Damn woman! Look what you did to my shirt!"

She giggled before turning her face severe. "Well, if you would quit pounding me with that thing, I would not have to do things like that." She hopped up and wiggled her buttocks over to get him a new shirt, Edward's eyes following every step.

She handed him the shirt and he kissed her deeply, their tongues probing, as his free hand squeezed her bottom.

Her hand slid down, her brain determining the best way to entice him to stay for a second round, when a knock sounded at the door.

This time, Edward's annoyance was real. "Who is it?" he bellowed.

"Philip, Sir Edward."

Edward released his wife and left the room, crossing to the door to the hall. He stepped into the hall and closed the door as Irina started to clean herself.

The English lord of Scottish lands looked down at his seneschal as he pulled on the new shirt. "What is so important?"

Philip knew his lord's temper and was aware that this was merely annoyance. "Lord Michael O'Brian of Kincora desires an audience with you, my Lord. He has your son Alexander with him."

Edward's eyes widened. "Michael's here?" Then his eyes went hooded. "And Alexander's with him. I wonder what the boy's done."

The door opened as he said the last. Irina arched an eyebrow. "My boy, I presume?"

Edward grinned sheepishly. "Apparently, dearest, he is your boy today."

She laughed as she laced her arm through his. "Well, Sir Edward, let's attend to our guest, and our son."

Lord Michael Mac Andrew O'Brian, Prince of the Dal Cais tribe and Master of Kincora, stood apart from the Scots that surrounded him in the great hall of Roslin. Behind him stood his wife Moira and his man-at-arms Padraig. Young Alexander stood between them.

Michael had not known of Alexander's parentage until minutes before and a small part of him worried what Sir Edward's reaction might be. They had been friends and comrades-in-arms, but that had been seven years before.

He saw Sir Edward and Lady Irina enter the hall and straightened. Edward stopped before the taller Irishman.

"Lord Michael."

"Sir Edward."

A moment of silence echoed in the hall as the two noblemen looked at each other. Without warning, a smile stretched Edward's bearded features and the two men embraced, shouting endearments and pounding each other's backs.

The two men stepped back and Edward caught a glimpse of the threesome behind the Irish knight. "And who are the two I am not acquainted with, old friend?"

"My Lord," the Irishman bowed low, a grin on his face, "may I present the Lady Moira, my bride, and Sergeant Padraig Mac Shane of Dublin, my closest confidant." Moira curtsied and Padraig bowed low, copying his master perfectly.

Michael put an arm around his old friend's shoulders and led him to the boy. "And this lad I believe you know."

Alexander looked around at the milling crowd, his face already red. The redness deepened when he spied Fiona, Brigid, and Anna entering, fresh from their swim. If Lord Michael told of his deeds now, they, and the rest of Roslin, would know. Alexander's eyes met Michael's and plead for silence.

"And what misdeeds have brought my son to your attention, old friend?"

The Irish knight's hawk-like eyes missed very little, and had also caught the entrance of the three girls from the lake. He felt that discretion would suit the boy's purposes best at this point.

"Perhaps, Sir Edward, we could discuss that in private."

The Englishman caught his hesitation but did not want to take issue with it. If the younger Irish warrior sought privacy for that discussion, he would have it. "Of course, Lord Michael."

Chapter 2

Alexander looked around the room nervously as Lord Michael described his afternoon travails.

While his wife had ridden in the carriage, Michael had scouted a little ways ahead. He had spied the three girls as he stopped his horse to wait for them to catch up. Minutes later, about the time they reached his spot, he saw the boy skulking along the path.

He dismounted and told them to wait before plunging into the forest. He discovered the hiding place where Alexander watched the women swimming and snatched him up.

Edward considered this, his face betraying no emotion. He looked over to the lad's mother. "The strap, wife?"

Neither the Earl or Lady of Roslin had even been of a mind to spare the proverbial rod. Irina appraised Alexander and detected the relief in his features. If the punishment were simple pain, he knew he could withstand it. A slight smile creased her lips. "No, husband. Let's just tell Fiona and her sisters what he was doing."

Something akin to panic seized the boy's features as he contemplated quickly the embarrassment of such a revelation. Alexander did not enjoy pain, but he had no urge to suffer such emotional distress as the hate-filled gaze he imagined Fiona would turn on him when the news was revealed.

Edward watched the play of emotions on his son's face with no small amount of amusement. Alexander was his second son and Irina his second wife. The boy was more like him by a large margin than his brother, which would make his request later t Michael even more difficult. But this had to be handled first.

The Earl of Roslin nodded decisively. "Good thinking, my Lady. Philip, fetch Anna, Brigid, and Fiona. Also, get Anna's husband John. He will want to know about the boy's spying as well." Philip turned to go, but Edward's voice stopped him. "Oh, and get their father, too. Knowing Peter, he will be hot as hell-fire, but it is only right." Philip nodded to the Earl and again turned to leave.

Alexander's panic was now very real, but a calm voice in his mind told him what he must do. "Please, father, mother, it will not happen again. I promise."

Philip stopped at the door and looked back at the scene, impressed by the boy's calmness.

Edward eyed his son. "You promise?"

"Yes, sir."

"You swear?"

"Yes, sir."

"Before Lord Michael as witness?"

Alexander glanced at the Irishman, whose green eyes were impassive. "I do, sir."

Edward nodded, contemplating, and looked at his wife. "What do you think, my dear?"

Irina smiled to herself. He was giving her the choice to be the bad guy. "I am satisfied with his sincerity, but he still needs punishment. Restrict him to his rooms for a week. He can only come out for meals and his lessons."

Edward's eyes were almost playful as he locked eyes with the Irish noble. "And you, old friend, what do you think?"

Michael nodded. "It sounds fair to me, Sir Edward."

Now Edward turned his blue eyes on his son. "It is done, then. Philip, escort the boy to his chamber."

The wives and servants had been sent away and wine was brought to drink. The comrades-in-arms drank and told jokes. And Edward and Michael remembered the battles they had fought.

The two warriors had met outside of Michael's stronghold at Kincora, where the Irishman's famed ancestor, the High King Brian Mac Kennedy of Boruma, had constructed his palace two hundred years before. A company from Leinster had decided to attack the Irish lord there. When his pleas for help had reached the court of King Henry, he had asked for a volunteer. The young Edward St. Clair had stepped forward.

Within two months, he had ridden before the gates of Kincora at the head of thirty knights and three hundred infantry. Lord Michael O'Brian, barely seventeen years of age, had ridden out to meet them, accompanied by two horsemen and a half-dozen men on foot. Michael had been as green as the surrounding countryside. Edward, without much in the way of experience himself, had been royal legate in Ireland.

The two men fondly reminisced about their first battle.

Sir Edward St. Clair, Earl of Clarence, Royal Legate to Ireland for His Majesty King Henry III, sat astride a powerful black horse, clad in chain mail under a red, black, and dark green tunic. A squire held his shield, white with a black engrailed cross, and a lance. The English knight's helm rested over the pommel of his saddle.

Lord Michael wore traditional Irish dress under thick leather armor. His tunic reached mid-thigh and left his legs bare. It was cinched at the waist with a gold belt. The sword he wore was of the old Viking tradition, purportedly taken form a Norse warrior by King Brian Boru shortly before his death at the Battle of Clontarf over two hundred years before. Surrounding Michael were two dozen foot soldiers armed with large battle axes. Standing beside Michael's mount was a spear-carrier named Padraig, holding a lance and shield.

The cavalry Edward had brought with him had been supplemented by a lighter cavalry force of Irish horsemen. Edward would personally command the cavalry while leaving the command of the infantry to Sergeant Eric Dawson, his most experienced foot soldier who had almost drooled at the sight of the axe-wielding Irish "heavy infantry".

The Englishman pulled out a spyglass brought back by a crusading compatriot and studied the army arrayed against them. The men from Leinster had about forty heavy cavalry and a large force of infantry. But Edward still did not see anything to counter his difference makers. As he watched, the Leinster infantry stepped out and began shouting insults at the combined forces of Munster and England.

Edward calmly raised his right fist and the forty men who had spent three hours a day practicing since arriving at Kincora stepped forward. They had been the greatest expense of the journey and Edward was convinced that they would be well worth it.

Their captain nocked an arrow, drew, and let it fly. Some of the Leinstermen stopped their insults and watched the flight. The unwitting target never saw it coming.

He was in the midst of suggesting irregularity in the parentage of his adversaries from Munster when the arrow struck his throat, neatly slicing through his trachea and jugular. A scarlet spray issued from the sliced vein and spattered his comrades. His lips continued to move as more blood flooded his mouth. Within moments, his sword fell from nerveless fingers as his bladder emptied and his bowels gave way. The light faded from his eyes as he dropped to the ground in a puddle of blood and waste.

The captain of the archers had not waited for the completion of the Leinsterman's death throes, but had turned to look down the double line of bowmen and started issuing orders in flat Welsh. He raised his right arm and the archers drew. When his arm dropped, forty arrows flew. His arm rose and fell again, and forty more arrows flew. Again and again, the Welsh captain raised and dropped his arm.

The Irishmen, both Munster and Leinster, had never seen anything like it. Within minutes, both sides had been introduced to the new realities of modern warfare.

The Leinster infantry fell in waves, cut to bloody rags by the Welsh bowmen. Some tried to run, but were still cut down as arrows struck their backs, severing arteries and spines and exposing brains to the bright Irish sun. The commander of the Leinster forces tried to rally his infantry, but to no avail as the survivors of the front ranks broke and ran.

Edward saw the opportunity he had been looking for and grinned. He could feel Michael's horrified eyes on him and made his voice cold as he called for his next wave with a single word: "Cavalry." With that, he pulled on his helmet.

The plan was simple. Edward would lead the heavy English cavalry in a frontal assault as Michael, relying heavily on his Marshal, Sir Eric O'Byrne, would lead the lighter Irish horsemen in a wide sweep into Leinster's left flank. Sergeant Dawson would trail the heavy cavalry at a trot, leading the Irish axemen as the spearhead to sweep up the remnants of Leinster resistance.

Edward took his shield and lance from his squire and stared at the opposite line. His men followed his lead as he began a thunderous charge. From the corner of the slit in his visor, Edward could see the Munster horse wheeling to the enemy flank. Their lesser force was countered by their greater speed. And as the Englishman had expected, the dual cavalry charge reached the Leinster cavalry at the same moment, causing even more chaos as they tried to re-form. Edward dropped his broken lance and drew his sword, parrying a strike from a mounted Leinsterman and severing his arm on a return stroke. As the Irishman screamed, the blade flashed across his lower face, cutting through jaw on its way to brain. Edward's horse wheeled as his eyes spotted a new target. He charged and slashed his new opponent across the back, slicing through his spinal column. He reared his horse as the Irish knight fell and was trampled, his skull crushed under heavy hooves.

Edward saw the Lord of Kincora spot the Leinster commander, who was beating a hasty retreat. Michael rode quickly after him, his Norse sword flashing in the sun. Edward rode after him as well.

The Leinsterman was accompanied by three knights. Two of them wheeled to face Edward and Michael. Michael faced off with the first one, who turned the Munster commander's back to his compatriot. Edward pulled his dagger and three it at the second man. A spray of red flashed from his throat, announcing his success. Michael's sword flashed and decapitated his opponent.

The comrades renewed their chase. Within moments, they had caught up to the Leinstermen. Edward took on the bodyguard while Michael squared off with the commander.

Edward fenced with the guard on horseback, analyzing the man's style and finding an opening. He feinted left and struck the guard's thigh with the flat of his blade. As the guard reacted to that move, Edward cut through his sword hand with a fore swing and through his throat with a backswing.

The Englishman swung his horse around and spotted Michael laying on the ground. The Leinster commander raised his sword, aiming a killing stroke at the boy's throat. Edward leaped from his horse, tackling the Leinsterman and driving his forearm into his adversary's temple. The Leinsterman fought back and rolled Edward onto his back. As he raised his fist, the Norse sword stuck out through his chest, a gout of blood shot out onto Edward's neck. Edward watched the commander die. As he pushed the body away, he took Michael's offered hand and got to his feet.

"Thanks," said the Irishman, who seemed to have aged ten years since the battle began.

The Englishman grinned. "Do not mention it, my Lord," he replied.

Chapter 3

The fire had burned down to embers and some of the candles had started to gutter.

The Irishman stood and stretched, still steady despite the amount of scotch whiskey he had imbibed. A couple of joints popped as he reached for the ceiling.

"Not that this has not been fun, Edward, but I can reminisce about battles past anytime. Why did you ask me to the fine hospitality of Roslin?"

The English lord looked up from a candle. "I have a difficult request to make of you, my friend."

Michael sat back down. "A serious request, I should expect?"

"Aye. It is."

"What is it, brother?"

"It is time for my Alexander to become a squire. There are plenty of knights, both around here and in England, who have offered, but none that I really trust."

Michael looked thoughtful. "I take it he is a handful."

"He can be rather difficult. Bt he is a good lad at heart. And he is quite bright."

Now, the Irishman chuckled. "Sounds like his father."

Edward joined his laugh. "Do not leave his mother out of that equation."

The men continued to grin. Michael looked the older warrior in the eye. "I will do it."

Michael opened the door to the suite of rooms provided for his retinue. He was immediately aware of Padraig's eyes alertly following him. The noble was sure that Padraig's hand gripped a knife, ready to draw the blood of an unexpected intruder. Michael could feel the tension leave his faithful servant as recognition dawned. Seconds later, the Lord of Kincora's footman and bodyguard's breathing had become deep and regular with sleep.

The Irish knight quietly crossed the room and entered the bedchamber. He quietly stripped and deposited his clothes on the floor. He padded across to the chamber pot and emptied his bladder of the night's revelry. He crawled into bed and slipped an arm around his wife's waist. His lips pressed softly against the spot where her neck joined shoulder and she stirred a little, pressing her naked bottom against his crotch for a moment.

Michael grinned and kissed her a little higher this time. The pressure in her response was greater this time and he reached up to brush the hair away from her ear before sliding his hand down to capture her diminutive breast. He took her earlobe between his lips and grazed it with his teeth. She reached back and took his stiff member in her hand, rubbing her thumb across the top.

Michael gasped and Moira chuckled as she pulled far enough away to roll onto her back. She pulled him atop her and he eagerly accepted the invitation, letting her hand guide him into her body. It was Moira's turn to gasp as he entered her. Their tongues tangled as they enjoyed each other's bodies, matching each other thrust for thrust. Finally, the heat and pressure radiating from his wife's body became too much and he gave a strangled cy as he climaxed. Between the alcohol and the sex, he nearly blacked out. Her movements beneath him and the pressure around his softening member brought him back to Earth as her fingers danced across her clitoris, bringing her own orgasm.

The Irishman held himself up as she moaned and shivered with pleasure. She gripped his upper arm as the waves of pure joy washed over her. When she was done and her breathing had returned to something resembling normal, he kissed her gently on the forehead and rolled off of her.

They laid next to each other, the sweat from their exertions cooling their bodies as it dried. The cool summer breeze through the window gave both of them chills in short order and Moira rolled onto her side, pillowing her head on her husband's shoulder. She felt his strong arm wrap around her until his hand rested on her buttocks. She grinned as she threw her leg over his and settled herself into the comfort of their usual sleeping arrangement. Her hand settled on his firm stomach and she closed her eyes as his breathing settled into the rhythm of sleep.

When she woke the next morning, Moira O'Brian was the last to wake. She had stirred when her husband had disentangled himself from her. She had heard him use the chamber pot and wash himself in the basin. He had been quiet in his dressing and leaving their bedroom, placing a kiss on her cheek and a pat on her bottom before departing. He was aware after four years of marriage that she took a little longer to get started than he.

She moved back the blanket she was under and sat up. Her eyes caught the reflection off the damp spot where they had lain the night before. Moira got out of bed and shivered violently at the sensation of cold stone under warm feet. She braved the floor to make her way to the chamber pot and squatted over it.

She chuckled as her bladder began to release. Unlike those women friends she shared intimate discussions with, she did not have to leave the warmth of her lover's arms to do this shortly after the act was done. But the morning after generally took longer than usual. This morning after was much the same.

Finishing, Moira took a linen strip and dried herself. She walked across to the wash basin and studied herself in the looking-glass above it. She was small, measuring five feet in height and weighing just a bit over one hundred pounds.. Her dark-brown hair hung below her waist and her deep brown eyes sparkled pleasantly. She had small, upthrust breasts that her husband admired adoringly and a petite bottom that he had trouble keeping his hands off of. Her hand trailed over her pubic mound and she frowned at the rough patch of stubble there. Shortly after their wedding, Michael had remarked at the thick mass of hair between her legs. She had been deeply distraught that night as he pleasured himself with his concubine and slept in her bed afterward. Her distress had grown as, despite the enticements of her fifteen-year-old body, he had continued to give his time to the older woman.

Moira knew that her marriage to Michael was a political alliance, but held out hope that the vigorous noble could be her regular lover and not have to share him. She had finally gathered the courage to confront Deirdre, her husband's concubine and her competition.

Deirdre leaned back on her bed and enjoyed the feel of her Lord's tongue caressing the depths of her vagina. He was talented, she thought, much more so than his older brother and far better than his father.

She reminisced at the memory of Lord Steven, Prince of the Dal Cais. She had been barely thirteen when she was brought to him, and, of course, a virgin. She had been left naked in his bed at Kincora, tears in her eyes from his violent invasion. She had been shocked at the blood puddling under her butt that dripped from the hairless slit between her legs. Then she had seen his semen oozing out of her. There was no telling how long she might have laid there had the plump old maid not come to get her cleaned up.

Deirdre felt her body quicken as Michael sucked gently on her clitoris then allowed his tongue to caress her opening and perineum.

Her mind drifted back to Renee's attentions. The older woman had bathed her, cleaning away the blood and semen from her deflowered hole before starting to fondle her gently. The plump Renee had undressed as well and Deirdre had sucked on her large nipples while Renee introduced her fully to orgasm.

Great flashes of pleasure brought her back. She curled her fingers into Michael's hair and tugged gently, barely able to contain herself. His tongue came away from her as he looked up past her flat stomach and small breasts. Her voice was husky with approaching pleasure. "Mount me, my Lord. Ravish me."

Michael needed no more encouragement. He climbed atop his lover and impaled her with one powerful thrust. Her moans of pleasure mounted to screams of joy as he drove himself into her tight confines. With a final thrust, he spent himself inside her. She squeezed him tight with her body and arms, her hands running over the scratch marks on his back as she milked him of every drop. They kissed and she licked her own juices off of his lips and chin.

He buried his face in her neck and hair to breathe in her scent. As she gazed, sated, over his shoulder, she saw the movement of a curtain and, hidden behind it, Michael's young bride of four months. She did not say anything as Moira again hid from view.

Michael pulled himself away from his lover and began to dress. "I am late!" he exclaimed, looking at the courtyard below the window as he tugged on his pants. Deirdre continued to lay there, marinating in their juices. Within minutes, he was gone, scooping up his Norse sword as he rushed away. After the door closed, her eyes tracked to the canopy above the bed.

"You may come out now, my Lady."

She sat up as Moira came out from behind the curtains and studied the girl. Deirdre felt a slight arousal at the obviously excited condition of Michael's wife. "I would ask why you are here," she began, "but it is fairly obvious."

Moira tried to look offended but could not pull it off. "It is?"

Deirdre nodded.

"Then why?"

Now the concubine smiled.

"You want to know why he comes to you occasionally to perform his husbandly duties and comes to me seeking pleasure."

Moira reddened, then nodded.

Deirdre grinned and walked a circle around the younger woman. "And you want to know why he would rather fuck my used-up old cunt than your fresh, young pussy."

She continued to circle Moira, who hesitated before looking down at the floor. Deirdre stopped behind the brown-haired beauty. She reached out to squeeze Moira's buttocks with both hands. The younger woman let slip a startled gasp that brought a delighted smile to Deirdre's lips. She smoothly wrapped her arms around Moira and squeezed her breasts, the nubs of her nipples hard against Deirdre's palms.

Deirdre loosened her blouse and pulled it over her head. She took the opportunity to run her hands over Moira's flat stomach. She loosened the younger woman's skirt and let it fall at her feet. She wasted little time with undergarments and Moira soon stood revealed as Deirdre studied her.

"Lesson one," began the concubine, "is that you must be comfortable with this." Deirdre moved her hands to indicate Moira's body. "I never wear clothes when I do not have to. I know I have given several guards and servants thrills, but I never concern myself with that. I am the Lord's concubine. None will bother me. More, you are his wife. And safer even than me."

Moira looked up at Deirdre and admired her form. The concubine was a little plumper in the hips and stomach, but otherwise was similar in shape. Moira noticed one major difference, though. She pointed at the tangled mass of pubic hair between her own legs. "What about this?"

Deirdre took her by the hand and guided her to a chair. "Sit back and relax, my dear. I will take care of that."

She opened a chest next to the chair and took out a pair of scissors. With quick snips, she trimmed the hair from around Moira's pubic mound. She then crossed the room to get a candle, putting it under some wax to heat. Deirdre then turned her attention to Moira's legs. She ran her hands over them, noting the fine hairs that were just dark enough to see. "Raise your arms," Deirdre commanded Moira. When she did, Deirdre looked revolted by the hair there. "Where are you from?" she asked.

"Derry. I am a princess of the Hy Neill."

"That explains it." She started to stir the wax.

Moira was too worried to notice the slight. "What is that for?"

"I am going to use this to remove the hair from your legs, armpits, and crotch."

The waxing process was painful and left Moira in tears curled in a ball on Deirdre's bed. Deirdre coaxed her into a tub, where Moira recovered for a time, listening to Deirdre's sexual wisdom. Deirdre then helped her dress and sent her away.

Before letting her leave, Deirdre gave Moira a long, deep kiss that was far more passionate than any she had shared with her husband.

After dinner, Moira returned to her chambers alone. She hesitated to do as instructed, but decided to follow Deirdre's orders. She stripped and looked at herself in the mirror. Her hands moved over her naked body. She crossed the room and began to fondle her breasts. It occurred to her that the Church would censure her for this, but she very much enjoyed the sensation.

She laid back on the bed, her thighs dampening with sweat. She had felt that before, when Michael's manhood throbbed against her. Her left hand reached down and she began to manipulate the folds of flesh between her legs. She touched the nub of her clitoris and gave a little jerk, gasping with the raw pleasure that gripped her system.

Her right hand pinched and rolled her nipple and she started to buck her hips a little as her arousal increased. Her left thumb massaged her clitoris as she pushed two fingers into her opening. Her moans grew in volume as she worked her body toward orgasm.

She was interrupted by a hand taking hers.

"What is this, bride?"

Moira was shocked at the sudden presence of her husband. She looked up at the big Irishman, whose eyes showed both amusement and arousal. He removed his tunic and kneeled at the foot of the bed.

Michael slid his hands under her bottom and learned in to kiss her swollen labia. Moira gasped at the feel of his lips, then his tongue against her bare vulva. His tongue pushed into her canal and her back arched as an intense wave of pleasure shot through her. Seemingly of their own accord, her hips bucked against him as her fingers squeezed her nipples. His lips moved up to her clitoris and he sucked it gently. She cried out as the first wave of her orgasm crashed against her.

Moira floated back to Earth to notice her husband smiling down at her, his member jutting out from beneath his muscular stomach. As he started to climb atop her, she put out a hand to stop him. She rolled him onto his back with a mind to try something Deirdre had talked about during her bath. She wrapped her hand around him and started to gently stroke it, drawing a pleased grunt from him. She kissed the tip, letting her tongue move around it. The bitter tang of his fluid mixed with the musky scent of his manliness to create a heady mixture that was pleasurably intoxicating.

Moira released him from her hand and sucked him into her mouth. She slid her lips up and down his shaft and his breathing shallowed. He growled low in his throat and his bitter juice flooded her mouth. She swallowed quickly as another burst followed. She held him there until he was done then crawled up to lay next to him.

"You are home early, my Lord." She picked up her head to find guilty eyes looking back at her.

He looked away after a moment. "I planned to spend the night with Deirdre. But she suggested I come to your bed instead."

Moira laid her head on his shoulder, kissing him there before doing so. "I spent the afternoon with her. We discussed many aspects of marriage. I think we have become friends."

Michael reached down and ran his finger over her smooth vulva. "I sensed she might have had something to do with this." His finger slid between her legs and gently pushed her button.

Moira could not help but moan at the pleasure it gave her. She saw him getting hard. Her voice was rough with desire. "Again, my Lord?"

He chuckled softly as he pulled her on top of his body. "Yes, my love," he said as his erection found the right spot and she sank down onto him.

Moira's hand slammed against the wall as her orgasm hit, the fingers of her right hand massaging the flesh between her legs. They were strong memories that gave her such pleasure. She used the linens to dry herself and began to dress.

Chapter 4

Quiet conversation buzzed around the room s the Lady of Kincora entered and found a seat on her husband's right. "Good morning, my Lady," he said softly.

"And to you, my Lord," she replied as a plate of beef sausage and eggs was set before her. She picked up a fork and began to eat.

Sir Edward sat at the head of the table, his seneschal at his right hand and his son at his left. The Lady Irina sat at the foot of the table with two of the ladies of Roslin attending to her. Irina dipped her head to Moira and Moira nodded back.

Michael leaned close to her and said quietly, "I forgot to tell you something last night."

She smiled at him. "Well, I did keep you distracted."

He squeezed her knee lightly. "You did a wonderful job of it, too."

They shared a quiet laugh. "What is this momentous news, my Lord?"

"We are taking young Alexander with us to Kincora. He will be my squire."

Moira nodded, chewing and swallowing a bite of eggs. "It is as you expected, then."

"As I hoped," he said.

"As you hoped."

Michael sipped at a mug of mead. "Sir Edward will make the announcement at court today."

Meanwhile, young Alexander remained unaware of the events swirling around him. He did not understand the distant sadness in his parents' eyes, so he dismissed it. Instead, his interest was held by the serving girl Fiona. He enjoyed the sway of her hips as she walked away and the gentle bouncing of her breasts when she came toward him. His mind recalled vividly the scene at the loch the day before, those breasts bared as she ran in the sunlight.

Alexander was distracted by the feeling of being watched. His eyes found those of Lord Michael and Alexander gulped hard. Michael pulled away and gazed at Fiona, studying her intently before looking back. A slight nod of the head passed between man and boy and Michael returned his attention to his breakfast.

Alexander was, to his surprise, pleased at Michael's approval at the object of his affection and turned back to his own meal.

Today would be a good day after all.

Irina stared silently out the window at the busy marketplace below. She hated the fact that her only child, the only one she would ever bear, was being sent away.

Alexander had been a bright-eyed, happy baby. There was obvious native intelligence in those green eyes and as he had grown older a sharp tongue and dry with that flustered many adults but entertained his parents. She saw that he would be find and strong, and she had caught the appraising glances tossed his way already by many prospective in-laws, and quite a few of the bolder unmarried women.

She had been quietly amused by his antics the afternoon before. It was good that he was interested in the pretty young things at court, and old Peter the Smith's daughters were fine examples of Scottish beauty. Both Fiona and Brigid were often watched by the men at court as they performed their duties. And Irina had caught Edward's eyes on Anna's plump bottom on several of her frequent visits to court. Irina had even heard some of the men comment that she would have no troubles finding a second groom if her much-older husband John Newcastle, the preeminent merchant in that part of Scotland, were to take ill and perish.

Indeed, Irina understood instinctively that Fiona would make a fine wife for her boy, if only her family was of noble blood. Irina knew that the pressures of society would never allow Alexander to marry for love, at least not the first time.

Her own husband had been married before, to Lady Eleanor Taggert, who had been the daughter o the Lord Mayor of London, Sir Louis Taggert. Eleanor had given birth to a son, Edward, who had been raised by the Taggert family after Eleanor's death. Only after her death did Edward go to tour his lands at Roslin, where he caught sight of the young Irina, daughter of a farmer, laughing with her friends at market.

It had not taken long for the handsome Earl of Roslin to entice the young woman to his bed, where her virginity was given to him freely. And for the first time, Edward St. Clair had enjoyed sex for the sake of love. Weeks later, Irina and Edward married. The next year saw the birth of Alexander after a hard pregnancy and delivery that left Irina unable to have more children. Little Alexander became the center of her universe.

And within the week, he would be gone to Kincora on the neighboring island. The mother wiped away the tears that streaked her face.

Brother Donovan had Alexander reciting scripture in Latin when Philip quietly entered the room. The saturnine seneschal was regarded by most he came in contact with as bookish and weak, the kind of man who should be saving souls, not taking lives. This could be a dangerous, even deadly mistake.

Philip had been a quiet youth growing up around the royal court at London. He was sent to Oxford to study for the priesthood, but, on a pilgrimage to Rome, discovered his true vocation.

Sweat cooled on Philip Le Clain's bare chest as he lay beside the naked girl. Physically satisfied, she had clung to Philip in he moments after their lovemaking. When her breathing deepened, Philip tenderly extricated himself from her embrace.

He pushed himself up on his elbow and looked at the face of his lover. Her long black hair framed a face of beauty that was marked by her mixed Spanish and Arabic heritage. Her name was Consuela Maria de la Cienega. Her father was a minor Spanish noble who trusted a drunkard of a Spanish knight to protect his daughter's virtue.

And her lover saw the irony that it was his perceived destiny to give himself body and soul to Christ. How am I going to give this up, he wondered. His finger traced around her nipple, causing it to pucker and eliciting a soft moan in her sleep.

It occurred to Philip that, if he played his cards right, he might get another go before he had to sneak back to his hut. But nature intruded on his thoughts as the urge to relieve himself became overpowering. He rose and pulled on his robe. He stepped around the snoring Spaniard in the outer room and slipped out of the hut and around the corner. He stepped into the relief hut and squatted over a bowl. He raised his robe and began to move his bowels. For the next several minutes, he contemplated the wall as he relieved his distress. When he was done, he used several strips of cloth beside the bowl to clean himself. He dropped the used linens in the pail by the door as he slipped back to Consuela's hut.

The first thing he noticed upon sliding through the door was the absence of the big Spanish knight. His concern grew as he stepped toward the door of her room and heard a rhythmic grunting. He opened the door and beheld in the lamplight Don Diego's half-naked body atop Consuela's naked form.

Philip was frozen in shock at the rutting Spaniard violating his lover from behind. Consuela was on her stomach, one of the big Spaniard's hands pushing her face into the blanket under her. With every savage thrust, she gave a muffled cry of pain and terror. With a final grunt and curse, he emptied himself into her. As he flooded her womb with his semen, Diego turned her head sharply, snapping her neck savagely. Then he collapsed on top of her.

The sound of Consuela's breaking neck galvanized Philip into action. He scooped the Spanish knight's dagger up and leaped onto him. He used the knight's shock and drunkenness to his advantage, yanking back on his hair and driving the dagger into the side of the thick neck. He forced the knife outward and a great gout of blood sprayed onto Consuela's dead body.

Philip held him down as he died.

The English cleric was woken by one of his traveling companions, who was in a thoroughly excited state.

"Brother Philip!" George's shaking brought Philip out of a bizarre dream. "Come quickly! It's murder!"

Philip scrambled from his bed and pulled a clean robe from his things. He pulled it over his head and was still tying it around his waist when he exited the hut.

Just outside the hut stood Herr Jakob, a severe Moravian knight with one eye who had become the de facto leader of their party. He stood with Brother Ian, the senior friar and Philip's other companion. They were locked in quiet, intense conversation. Finally, Herr Jakob nodded sharply and turned away from the tall, thin Englishman.

Jakob looked at the milling crowd. "All right, everyone, back to your huts. Prepare to continue our journey." As the others broke up, Herr Jakob scurried away to speak to the sallow fellow that Philip recognized as the local magistrate. Philip then saw Brother Ian waving him and George over.

"Brother George, prepare our belongings for an afternoon departure." George nodded and hurried off to do Ian's bidding. The older man looked over at Philip and jerked his head toward the hut. Philip followed him in.

The harsh sunlight revealed stark detail that had remained hidden the night before. Don Diego's body had been moved off of Consuela, who had been flipped onto her back. The look of shock frozen on Diego's face was almost comical. The look of terror on Consuela's was painful to see. Philip realized that it had been love he had felt for her, not the mere lust that he had given into with several women that had passed through his life. Now came the cold fact that she was gone and a tear welled up in his eye.

Ian had his back turned on the tableau. "Interesting lack of reaction, considering how you must have felt about her."

Philip looked up. "What?"

Ian's grin was not pretty. "This is not my first time around a dead body. I was a sergeant in the Order of Teutonic Knights. I left that Order five years ago. There was too much killing. Now I finally leave the monastery to go on pilgrimage and I end up traveling with a killer."

Philip was stunned.

"You have been leaving our accommodations over the last fortnight and visiting Consuela's bed. I figure you found them last night, surprised them, and killed them."

"No," Philip mumbled.

Ian's gaze locked on Philip. "Then, what happened?"

Philip reached out and touched Consuela's hair tenderly. "We were together last night. I just realized that I had really fallen in love with her. I wanted to run away with her."

Ian's gaze had not softened.

"I left her to relieve myself. When I got back, I found Don Diego raping her. In his lust, he killed her. And I killed him, with that dagger." He pointed at the blade on the floor. "I took my robe and buried it in the rubbish, then I washed and got into bed."

"Did you sleep?"

"Yes." Philip was surprised by the question.

Now Ian nodded. "Good. You are a born killer. I will not turn you over to the magistrate. You will complete the pilgrimage and leave the Order when we return to London. You do not have the temperament for it anyway. I will introduce you to men who will further your education in the arts of murder and secrecy. You will serve nobles for the rest of your days, and you will be judged by the Almighty at their close.

"Your days of serving God are over."

Philip had finished the pilgrimage. He had been to Rome and toured the world of Caesar and Augustus, then returned to London. Ian had, indeed, introduced him to several of those who operated behind the scenes in London's royal court. They had taught him the arts of murder, how to kill with poison, the stiletto, and garrote of Italian tradition. They were arts he had employed often in those years, and he had never been caught, never been harmed, never even suffered a sleepless night or one beset by nightmares.

He had never again tasted of love like he had found for Consuela. He had known lust in the arms and beds of many women, even many married women, over the years. And, after he had served five years in the employ of King Henry III, he had sworn his loyalty to the young Sir Edward St. Clair, then Earl of Clarence, who had just married the daughter of Sir Louis Taggert. And now, he had work.

Philip cleared his throat softly. Brother Dominic looked up from his tome and young Alexander merely looked curious. "Young Lord," began the seneschal, "your father requires your presence in his hall. He has an announcement to make regarding your future."

Alexander could not help but look happy to be getting away from his lessons for the second day in a row, but neither Philip nor Dominic could do anything about that.

Sir Edward St. Clair looked around his hall. Many had gathered quickly at the news of the impending announcement. Lord Michael O'Brian and his Lady Moira stood across the room from him, Michael dressed in the traditional kilt of his clan. Edward grinned to himself at this display of the Irishman's finery. Michael liked to brag that his ancestors had taken to wearing pants even as the Scots wore kilts. But Michael understood the traditions of Celtic blood.

Irina came to Edward's side as Philip brought in Alexander. They wasted no time in presenting themselves at the Earl of Roslin's side. Sir Edward stood and conversation came to a quick stop.

"As many of you know, my boy Alexander has reached the age of his proper training as a nobleman and a knight. You also know that we are being graced with the presence of Lord Michael O'Brian, Prince of the Dal Cais tribe, Lord of the Irish land of Thomond, and a Prince of Munster. Lord Michael is also one of my closest allies and dearest friends. I have long considered him a brother.

"Lord Michael and I discussed these arrangements last night and came to an agreement. My son Alexander will depart with Lord Michael and Lady Moira at the end of the week and will return with them to Kincora. He will spend the next several years there in training for military and noble service. When he has completed his training to both Lord Michael's and his satisfaction, he will be invited to return to Roslin, where he will take his proper place at my right hand. From today onward, he will formally be heir to my lands at Roslin."

Silence reigned in the hall as the information was digested. Then applause broke out.

Lord Michael made his way across the room and put an arm around young Alexander. He looked down at the lad, who seemed somewhat stunned by the turn of events. "Will that do, boy?"

Alexander looked up at the big Irishman, more than a little intimidated. "Aye, my Lord," he managed to come out with.

Happy or not with the turn of events, Friday saw the Irish spear-carrier Padraig loading goods and preparing the horses for departure. Finally, he led out Boruma, Lord Michael's proud stallion, and an equally-proud black mare that had been given to Alexander as a going-away present. He bowed deeply as Lady Moira O'Brian and Lady Irina St. Clair came out of the hall.

The two women, who had become fast friends, embraced each other. There were tears as they parted. Sir Edward led Lord Michael and the young squire Alexander out to the carriage. Irina hugged her son and kissed him on the cheeks. Edward embraced his son and his friend before they mounted their horses. Padraig pulled himself up onto his seat.

Lord Michael admired the powerful mare that Alexander sat astride. "A beautiful creature, as I told your father. What is her name?"

"I have not named her, my Lord." Alexander was still intimidated by the Irishman.

Michael laughed. "You must, before we leave, lad. We can not have a horse running around with such an important charge that does not have a name."

Alexander looked around. "What would you name her, my Lord?"

Michael patted the horse's mane. "She reminds me of the stories of my ancestor's mare. She was a proud horse that carried the Ard Ri of Ireland."

"Ard ri?"

"That's ancient Irish for 'High King', lad. My ancestor was the great Brian of Boruma, the last true king of a united Ireland."

Now, Alexander smiled, liking the sounds of the Irishman's tale. "And what was his horse's name?"

Michael's eyes veritably shone with pride. "Briar Rose."

Alexander nodded. "Then, with your permission, my Lord, I will call her 'Briar Rose' in honor of your ancestor."

"I would be proud of that, Alex."

And with that, a friendship was forged between Irish Lord and Scottish squire.

Chapter 5

The sun had finally broken through the fog in Roslin. Fiona stepped out of her cottage and looked up at the luminous disk. She closed her eyes as it warmed her face. She heard a branch snap as the three men came out of the forest.

The one in the middle was an obvious leader. He had rakish good looks and a dagger stuck in his belt that was obviously sharp. The muscle was on his right. His Nordic heritage was betrayed by his blond hair and broad shoulders. His big hands were attached to thick arms and his legs were the size of tree trunks. He wore no shirt and his chest was hairless and extremely muscular. The boy on the leader's left was plainly excited by the prospects that had presented themselves on this fine Scottish morning. His boyish charm was offset by the bulge in his trousers.

The leader bowed low like a courtier. "Allow me to introduce myself. I am Derrick and I and my compatriots wish nothing more than a fine breakfast and to pay you with the only coin we have." His eyes tracked to the boy on his left. "And that's to show you a good time this fine morning."

Fiona's eyes had already tracked to Sean and Myra's cabin, which showed a disturbing lack of life this morning. Her mind, which was on the verge of panic, recalled that they had gone to Edinburgh to visit Myra's family. Fiona was alone. She shot away in a dead run.

Her speed was nothing to Derrick, who was on her in moments. As his fellows caught up with them, Derrick knocked her to the ground and pinned her there. His hands went to her blouse and tore it open, exposing her breasts to the cool morning air. She could feel his hardness as he pressed her to the ground. Next his hands moved to her skirt. He was pulling it up, his companions laughing at the conquest, the young one rubbing his erection through his pants, when a dark shadow fell across them.

A sickening crack rang out as one booted foot caught the younger one across the chin, snapping his jaw and displacing several teeth. His head snapped back with the force of the blow. All eyes tracked to his attacker, who sat astride a magnificent white stallion.

The mounted figure was obviously tall and well-dressed. He had long, strawberry-blond hair that was pulled back into a ponytail. He was also clean-shaven with a long, white scar that traveled across his left jaw line. A tartan kilt covered his legs and fine leather boots encased his feet. A brown tunic covered his chest and a cloak that matched his kilt was over his shoulders. With a flash, he drew a fine broadsword from a scabbard on the horse's saddle.

His voice was harsh and flavored with a fine Scottish brogue. "You have two choices now, lad. You can pick up your mate and his teeth and disappear, or you can face my justice."

With a quickness that belied his excessive girth, the giant clubbed the horseman's sword hand and grabbed him from the saddle, tossing him easily to the ground. With the grace of a powerful cat, the horseman rolled through the throw and came back up to his feet. With a swift slice of his left hand, a newly-drawn dagger cut away a slice of the behemoth's cheek. When the big blonde's hand went to his bleeding face, the warrior's foot fired into his left knee. The giant fell to his pained knee and another slice traversed his throat, slicing two jugular vessels and his windpipe, spraying blood from his gaping neck. The Norseman was definitely surprised as the light died from his eyes.

The horseman looked at the stunned Derrick. "He's made his choice. Now, what's yours?"

Derrick leaped at the man with the dagger, drawing his own from his belt. An easy sidestep and the horseman was away from danger. He moved like a dancer and placed himself between Fiona and Derrick. "Who the hell are you?" hissed Derrick.

A grin creased the horseman's face. "Sir," was all he said.

Derrick tried a quick slice, which the laughing knife-fighter danced easily away from.

"What?"

The horseman was obviously enjoying himself as he feinted left and cut right, slicing tendon's in Derrick's left wrist. "I believe your question should have been, 'Who the hell are you, Sir?'."

Another quick move brought a cut across Derrick's right forearm. Derrick screamed in frustration and stabbed at the retreating horseman. With a quick move, he spun inside the arc of Derrick's blade and stabbed directly into Derrick's heart. "Sir Alexander," he whispered as Derrick's blood spilled the ground between them and he died with a curse still on his lips.

Alexander pulled his dagger from Derrick's chest and dried it on the brigand's shirt. He sheathed it and pulled his cloak from his shoulders. He handed the cloak to Fiona, pointedly looking away from her beautiful breasts. He picked up his fallen sword and stowed it in the scabbard on his horse's saddle. Then, he picked up the boy from where he lay, sobbing through his broken jaw. The knight pulled the boy up to his eye level.

"When you can talk again, boy, tell your friends and compatriots that Sir Alexander St. Clair has returned to claim his rightful place as Earl of Roslin. Tell them also that any bandit or brigand who believes he can harm my people with impunity will face my sword and my justice. The only end to their path is death. Tell them." He released the boy, who held his shattered jaw and ran away into the forest as easily as he could. The big Scottish knight turned back to Fiona.

"Fiona, my dear, it is not safe for you out here. Go get dressed and come with me."

Fiona found herself obeying without conscious thought. In all honesty, she was still dazed from the morning's events. She also recognized that the handsome boy who'd always acted shy around her had grown into a strong, capable, and handsome, man. It would be an adventure to find out how the rest of the day went.

Philip stood in front of the great hall as the deputation of horsemen rode through. The man in front wore the plaid of the St. Clair family while a trailing horseman carried the shield of St. Clair, with its engrailed black cross on a white background. The leader looked severe as he entered the gate.

Then his green eyes found Philip and a broad smile creased his face. He jumped down from the horse and embraced the smaller Englishman. "Lord Alexander?" asked the cleric with the assassin's training.

"Of course, Philip. It's me." The excitement in the twenty-two-year-old's voice was plain. Philip actually had to fight not to show the same feeling. He did allow a small smile to appear on his face.

"My Lord, I am pleased you have arrived home." He bowed deeply to the new Earl of Roslin. "And I am not the only one who has been waiting for you."

"Lord Alexander!" shouted a gruff voice from behind Philip. The bearer was a large, bearded man who stood in the doorway to Roslin's great hall.

"That is not who I meant, Sire." Philip's distaste was plain on his face, but he made himself smile as he turned. "My Lord, allow me to present Duke Malcolm Bruce, cousin to Prince Robert Bruce." Malcolm was the man who had called to Alexander. His companion was tall and slender. "And Earl Edwin Stanton, kinsman to John Balliol."

Malcolm embraced Alexander with gusto while Edwin contented himself with a handshake. Alexander was well-acquainted with the disagreements over the Scottish throne and that Balliol and Bruce were the two top contenders. Rumor had it that John Balliol had pledged his allegiance to the English King Edward, better known as "Longshanks". In return, Edward, and more importantly his great and well-trained army, would support Balliol's claim. This drove more Scotsmen into Robert Bruce's camp every day, for they could not stomach the idea of a turncoat king.

Alexander made himself listen to the two representatives' discussion for a few minutes before politely extricating himself from the discussion. He approached Philip, who was a few feet away and busy making arrangements for Alexander's retainers and their horses to be fed and housed. He got the seneschal's attention. "Who were you talking about then, Philip?"

Philip grinned and, with a flip of his head, led Alexander into the great hall.

There stood Fiona talking to a still-beautiful Irina St. Clair. Alexander had to restrain himself from running to her but still took a quick gait across the room. His arms encircled his mother and he picked her up off of the floor, spinning around with her in his arms. He heard her startled gasp and heard it turn into happy laughter. "My boy!" she cried into his ear as tears of happiness ran down her face.

He put her down and held her at arm's length, looking at his mother's tear-streaked face and laughing smile. She pulled him to her this time and held his large frame while she laughed further.

Alexander smiled over his mother's shoulder at Fiona and the glint of a tear in her eye. It was good to be home.

"Did Father support the Bruces or the Balliol claim?"

Philip sat across the table from Alexander. After a short reunion with his mother, Alexander had sat down to lunch with his father's seneschal. The two had dined on chunks of roast mutton and carrots with bread. Glasses of French wine had been emptied and refilled on a few occasions. Philip was impressed with how much the new Earl of Roslin could put away of the strong concoction.

"Well," Philip said after swallowing the latest forkful of meat, "in his heart, I believe he supported the Bruces. But, he was an Englishman, and it is well known that Balliol has Edward Longshanks' backing. So, openly, at least, he supported John Balliol. In fact, Balliol will be here for an evening meal in two weeks' time."

Alexander nodded. "I was afraid that when I returned, I would have to fall into Scottish royal politics." He sighed. "It was easier fighting Irish bandits in the backcountry, or French forces that opposed their king."

Philip chuckled. "I believe that very easily, Sire."

Chapter 6

Alexander was surprised to find Fiona and his mother together. It was obvious that they had been catching up. Alexander grinned at the two women and took the opportunity to study them.

Irina looked little different than she had before. She was still his mother, a little thicker in the waist, a few more crinkles around her eyes, a little more gray in her hair. But her eyes were still full of love for her son and her lips were still creased in a smile that was glad to see him.

Fiona, on the other hand, had just grown more perfect than Alexander's mind could recall. Her breasts, whose nakedness Alexander had noticed that morning, were full and firm. Her hips were broad below her trim waist. Her full reddish-blond hair hung to her waist and framed a heart-shaped face with full lips and green eyes that spoke to the man that Alexander had become. As the two women rose and came to greet him, the Earl of Roslin could not help but notice the provocative sway of her hips as she came toward him. Behind his mother's back, her eyes continued to suggest the pleasures that her body could share with his. The Scottish knight fought to control his desires as his mother reached to embrace him.

In an instant, he was transported to the best days of his childhood as his mother folded him into her hug. Irina pulled his head down to her shoulder and cried as she kissed his hair. "I am so happy to see you, my son," she whispered to him and he squeezed her tighter.

She finally released him but held onto his hand and led him to the chairs next to the fire. Alexander was a little dazed that Fiona took his other hand. They sat him in the middle chair, facing the fire, and took chairs at his side. "So, my son," began his mother after motioning for ale for the three of them, "tell me about your squire-ship at Kincora."

Alexander nodded slowly, gathering his thoughts. He had not been able to write much, even though he knew that Lord Michael had written regularly to his father. "First, tell me what happened to my father."

The glint of a tear shone in his mother's eyes as she contemplated the tale. "He was fine a year ago, son," she began. "In November, he came down with a cough. It was bad. He coughed up blood, even though he tried to hide that. He called Philip regularly to bring cures from the townswomen. But Brigid kept me informed of his problems even as he tried to hide bloody handkerchiefs from me. He worsened around Christmas, but improved after. Then he took a severe downturn. He was gone in April."

Alexander looked questioningly at Fiona. "Brigid?" She nodded. He wondered momentarily why Fiona's sister would know so much about his father's condition, knowing that Edward would have stayed completely faithful to his loving wife and that Irina would never be friendly to a mistress of the man she loved.

The knight turned back to his mother. "Why was I never informed?"

"He would not allow it. Your father remained proud to the end. It took an act of the Almighty to get Philip to write you a bare two weeks before his death. He barely let me know how you were doing. But he was very proud of your knighthood and of your prowess in battle. He veritably glowed when he talked about your fighting for King

Philip in France. I know that Lord Michael was going to take you on pilgrimage to Rome in a year, but this happened." She looked away from Alexander's glistening eyes.

Alexander held her close as she began to cry.

The new Earl of Roslin stood on a battlement along the wall his father had added over the years. The wall was far from the tallest he had stood on, or even attacked, in the ten years since he'd left Roslin. Still, there was something endearing about this particular wall. He turned and looked into the compound protected by these walls.

The market in the center of the castle was closing for the night. The blacksmith was lowering the heat in his forge while the butcher closed a pair of pigs in his pen for the night. The small guard force that would patrol through the night would protect any wares left outside the shacks that made up the market. The village priest stood outside the church but would soon retire to his parsonage for the night, where his maid would fix his meal and prepare his clothes for the next day. From Philip, he had learned about the smith's apprentice, the teenage boy who would slip out of his bed to spend regular nights with the priest..

Alexander walked down the steps from the wall and stopped at the gate, where the Marshal, Seamus McKilbride, snapped to attention and sketched a salute. "At ease, Marshal." Alexander could not hide a slight grin.

"Thank you, Lord Alexander." Whatever else you said, Seamus was all business.

"Any problems?" asked the Earl.

"No, sire, none we plan on, but all we prepare for."

Alexander nodded. "Good," he said, bowing slightly before heading for the main hall.

It certainly was quiet as Alexander stepped into the great hall. The courtiers, such as they were, had slipped out for the night, the latest court intrigues no doubt having taken a break for the night. The young Earl of Roslin caught sight and hearing of Earl Edwin Stanton in quiet argument with Philip. He also saw Brigid watching intently from across the room. He took the opportunity to observe Fiona's younger twin. She had changed little from the girl in his memory. Her face had hardened somewhat, an effect that was not unattractive, and she had kept the slenderness that she had always had. He still wondered about the intent looks that were passed to Philip from her. He was so intent on his observation that he never heard the intruder approach.

"I hoped it would be me you looked at with such intensity."

Fiona had snuck up on him and surprised him completely. He was flustered a bit at her charge, but saw the sparkle in her eye that told him it was at least partly a joke. He grinned back at her after seeing that neither Philip's conversation or Brigid's watching of it had been disturbed. "I did not want your sister to feel left out."

She looped her arm around his and led him away from the main room of the great hall. "You did not eat your supper, sire."

He chuckled. "I was not hungry," he protested.

"Nonsense," she said, "besides, you need your strength. You are the Earl of Roslin now. Your people need you strong."

Alexander quit his protesting as she squeezed his arm and led him into a small dining area where she had set a table for him. Roast pork was in a warming basin with potatoes and carrots while a chilled ale had been poured into a mug for him. "Was this just in case you found me wandering around the hall?"

She chuckled at him. "I stacked the deck by checking with Philip as to your location before I brought it in here. He said you were going up to the wall to look out. I was heading out there when I found you."

He nodded back. "Very nice." He sat down at the table and picked up a fork. He speared a chunk of pork and ate it, chewing it slowly. "Did you make this?"

Her smile was one of pride. "Yes, my Lord. I made it especially for you. Irina told me it was one of your favorite dishes when you were a child."

He laughed after he swallowed. "It still is."

Fiona played waitress while Alexander cleaned his plate and drank two full mugs of ale. He was happily full when he leaned back in his chair. Fiona took his dishes away and returned to lean on the table before him. "So, my Lord, are you going to tell me about your adventures?"

Alexander contemplated the woman before him. There was no mistaking her intentions. "Certainly." He stood. "But not here." He boldly reached out and took her hand. She did not resist as he led her out of the small room and down the hall to his chambers. He pulled her into his room and closed the door behind them.

Her arms snaked around his neck as he pushed her back against the door. Their lips locked together and she moaned as he pressed his body against hers. She could feel his throbbing hardness against her belly and her own dewy moisture gathering between her legs. She tugged at his tunic, pulling it up and over his head to expose his hard chest and abdomen to her hands. Her lips caressed him and sucked at his nipples.

His own hands pulled at her dress, pulling it away from her body until she stood naked in his arms. His hands slid to her firm bottom and then to her muscular thighs. Her left leg lifted up and he moved his hand up to her well-lubricated opening. She gasped into his mouth as he stimulated her, locating the nub of her clitoris and deftly massaging it as her fluids flowed over his fingers. She unwrapped his kilt and dropped it to the floor while her fingers explored his thick, hard member.

He lifted her off of the floor and pushed her back against the door. She slipped her hand between them and again found his throbbing member. She stroked him as he positioned her properly. She held him still as he lowered her onto his erection. She pulled her lips away from his and gave off a low moan as he penetrated her. Her hand wrapped around his neck as he stuffed her full of his manhood. She crossed her ankles at the small of his back and she used the muscles of her feet and legs to ride him.

Small explosions started behind her eyes and she groaned as her clitoris rubbed against his pubic bone. She knew that neither of them would last long. He held her against the wall and began driving into her with a force she had never felt in her life. She did not even realize that it was her voice crying out his name as her orgasm washed over her. As she floated back to Earth, she could hear short grunts from Alexander's mouth. He held them both against the wall as he kissed her neck and collarbone.

Fiona sighed as she uncrossed her ankles and set her feet on the floor. As his softening member slid from her engorged vagina, she could feel their mixed fluids running out of her body. She reached down and cupped the fluids against her opening. Alexander released her and she stumbled to the anteroom where the chamber pot waited. She let her body unclench and released her bladder into the bowl. She felt his semen and her fluids run down as well. She dried herself with a linen strip and walked more assuredly toward the bed, where Alexander already rested. She laid her head on his shoulder and sighed contentedly.

"I always knew I would end up here, Alexander."

Alexander laughed softly and kissed her on the head. "Fiona, I think I have wanted this longer than you have."

She pushed herself onto an elbow and pressed her breasts against his side. "How long would that be?"

He grinned. "For a long time."

"Before or after you used to watch us bathe in the loch?"

Alexander was a bit disturbed at the knowledge that she knew about his excursions. "Before. And how did you know?"

"You were not the quietest hunter. I used to watch you watching Anna and Brigid. It got me quite aroused, love." As she said the last sentence, her hand reached for his flaccid penis. She wrapped her long fingers around its base and squeezed gently. She dipped her head over it and used her tongue to prod it back to life.

He moaned deeply as she took the head into her mouth. She sucked gently, like a child at a teat. It took mere seconds for it to thicken to its full size. She took it into her mouth, her tongue massaging the underside of his full erection.

He pulled her away from her fellatio and plunged his tongue into her mouth, moving over her body. She wasted no time in guiding him into her again-moistening opening. She gasped as he drove it into her for the second time in thirty minutes. She dug her fingers into his shoulders and pulled him against her.

After several minutes, she climaxed again. Slightly less intense, but no less pleasurable, she settled down to realize that Alexander had not shared in her wonderful orgasm. She settled a hand against his chest and kissed him gently. He slowed his thrusting and she rolled him onto his back, holding on to settle on top of his peak. She rocked gently back and forth as he pushed himself into her. She looked into his eyes as he worked himself into a frenzy.

Fiona felt her lover's orgasm arrive as he injected her with his seed. She smiled down at him as she watched a look of intense joy and pleasure wash over his face. She laid her head on his chest as his ejaculations lessened and he finished inside her. She leaned up to kiss him on the lips.

Within minutes, he was asleep beneath her. Seconds later, she joined him.

Chapter 7

Alexander's hand stretched out to find the spot beside him empty. He moved his hand around, continuing the search, as his eyes opened. He sat up to find himself alone in his bed. The disappointment was not a pleasant feeling. Then he remembered the pleasant feeling of Fiona beneath him and on top of him, surrounding him with her womanhood. For a moment, he became aroused again, his erect penis reminding him of an intense need to urinate. He hopped out of bed and padded over to the chamber pot. As he relieved himself, he heard the door to his chambers open.

He peered back over his shoulder to see Fiona carrying a tray of bread and ale. She looked at the bed, puzzled, before her ears detected the sound of him in the bathroom. He saw the look of joy when she saw him and was warmed at her reaction. She set the tray down and undressed.

He finished and shook himself dry. She met him at the door and kissed him deeply, stretching her hand down to touch him as their tongues met, writhing against each other like two snakes. She caressed him as he hardened and his hand closed over one of her firm breasts, feeling the point of her nipple against his palm. She giggled as she pulled away. "I am hungry," she laughed.

He grinned back, squeezing her round bottom. "Me, too."

Her hand smacked his bottom in response. "For food."

With that, she wiggled her bottom at him as she walked back to the bed and selected a hunk of bread and used a knife to spread butter on it. Alexander crossed to stand next to her and began to eat another hunk of bread dry. She settled on the bed and laid back, watching Alexander watch her. She knew she was beautiful and, if she had doubted it, Alexander's reaction to her naked body proved it to her.

He laid down next to her and handed her a glass of ale. She sipped from it and handed it back. He set it down and leaned over to kiss her. Again, they kissed deeply. This time, she did not pull away as his hand moved to fondle her breast. She moaned into his mouth as his fingers gently twisted her nipple. Her moans deepened when his hand slid down over her stomach and past her silky pubic hair to find her moist slit.

His fingers played with the nub above her opening and she squirmed with pleasure. He did not relent as his fingers worked their way into her body. Her hand found his hard manhood and she began to caress him. His fingers worked her over, sliding in and out of her body as she stroked him, feeling fluids leaking over her fingers.

Her rhythm broke as she climaxed, her back arching and her breasts pressing against Alexander's hard chest. She forced herself to focus and resumed her stroking as Alexander's fingers relaxed. She nipped at his tongue and he pulled his head back, groaning with pleasure. She pushed him onto his back with her other hand and picked up the pace with her hand. Her head dipped down and she closed her lips over the head of his erection as he reached his own orgasm. His bitter fluid flooded her mouth and she swallowed reflexively. The second squirt was less full and she held him in her mouth as he finished, swallowing at the end of his climax.

She looked up over his flat belly and hard chest and smiled at the relaxed look on his face. She found herself tired as she laid her head on his shoulder and kissed his chest.

His arms enclosed her as his breathing deepened. She heard him fall asleep and joined him a moment later.

When Fiona awoke, she knew it was mid-morning by the sun. She kissed Alexander awake and he smiled at her. She reached past him and took a long drink from the ale by the bedside. "Good morning, my Lord," she smiled at him.

He squeezed her and kissed her again. "It has been so far."

She giggled. "Yes, it has." She pulled his hand to her mouth and inhaled the scent of her own womanhood before gently kissing his fingers. She released his hand and finished the ale with another drink. She set the glass down and settled herself against her lover.

"I have been meaning to ask," began the new Earl of Roslin, "why you haven't been married. Or have you?"

She looked away for a moment. "I have. I married Malcolm Mac Bain about a year after you left."

"I did not see Malcolm around the farm."

"He died four years ago."

"That would explain it. I am sorry to bring it up."

She smiled at him. "It is all right, Alexander. The marriage was to help my family, not for love."

"So, you're not involved with anyone now?" His hopefulness was plain on his face.

She kissed him. "Just you."

He smiled at her.

She was curious herself. "Why haven't you married yet, love?"

His smile turned wry. "I am keeping myself open to a dynastic alliance. Plus, I'm still young. Or I might hold myself open to marrying for love."

Now Fiona turned serious. "No, you need to further your family's fortunes. Love can come later."

"I'm surprised you would say that."

"I worry for you, not myself. You can have me anytime you want. I am in love with you and I believe I always have been. I'm just glad you returned to Roslin. But you need to focus on the future of your line. Search out a bride of royal blood, one of the Bruce's cousins or one of Balliol's clan. I will always be here for you."

Alexander was touched by Fiona's concern, especially as it came at her expense. He squeezed her to him and kissed her lips gently. "I love you, Fiona."

She traced the scar along the edge of his face with her finger. "And I you, Alexander."

Philip met his Earl as he strode into the great hall. The seneschal had been watching Malcolm Bruce and Edwin Stanton all morning, ever since the news had come in that morning that King Edward Longshanks would be sending his army to tour Scotland in support of John Balliol.

Malcolm and the other Bruces were no doubt concerned as to the amount of control Longshanks wanted over the nation of Scotland. There were rumblings throughout Scotland about rebellion in the face of Balliol's kowtowing to the English king. Philip crossed the room in mincing steps to meet Alexander.

"My Lord," he bowed to his old friend's son.

Alexander was obviously more chipper than he had been the morning before at his arrival at Roslin. Obviously, Brigid's intelligence had been good. The new Earl of Roslin nodded in response to the bow.

"Good day, Philip. How go the affairs of Roslin?"

"Very well, sire. Both Malcolm Bruce and Edwin Stanton want a private word with you."

Alexander's good mood dimmed considerably. "I thought they might. All right, I'll meet with Stanton before lunch and Bruce after. Will that satisfy them and their princes?"

Philip sketched down the details. "I am sure that will, my Lord. I will inform them."

As Philip skittered away, Alexander's eye caught Fiona talking with her twin sister Brigid. He admired his new lover for a moment before being interrupted by Philip. "Earl Edwin will meet with you presently and Duke Malcolm will do the same after lunch."

Philip caught the Earl of Roslin's eye tracking toward Fiona and Brigid and sighed, a slight grin on his face.

"Beautiful, eh, sire?"

It took Alexander's brain a moment to work out the logic as Philip slipped away. The truth dawned on him as Brigid's eyes focused on Philip's sidling gait. Philip and Brigid were lovers.

Chapter 8

Earl Edwin Stanton, Lord of Wallingsford and Plankstown in the Scottish highlands, reminded Alexander of a serpent who had grown legs. His hair was straw-colored and slicked back on his head. He had a long face matched by a long neck. He wore a tartan kilt and plaid of the Balliol clan. An expensive cloak covered this and trailed down to his legs. He looked almost distastefully at everything that surrounded him. It was, altogether, hard to like him if you were a Scottish noble that was proud of being a Scottish noble. Indeed, everything about him reeked of the assumed superiority of the English claim over Scotland.

Even his accent was more English than Scottish as he told Alexander, "My Lord Alexander, let me guarantee you more strength under the rule of John Balliol. I can promise lower taxes, even lower tithes, and more lands. King Edward of England has promised great lands in the south for those who will swear openly to follow the Balliol clan. He has even hinted at granting those loyal nobles the right of *prima nacta*."

Alexander's head snapped up, a blank look on his face. It was a look that might have been considered dangerous by the more intelligent. "*Prima nacta*?"

Edwin grinned. "Yes. Imagine, sire, the right to bed every virgin in your lands on her wedding night. Just the thing a powerful young lord like yourself would cherish, unless I miss my guess."

Alexander laughed deep in his throat. "Fresh, sweet, young things with plump thighs and breasts taken by me on their wedding night? Yes, what else could a powerful young lord like me want?" It was obvious to Alexander that Edwin could not sense sarcasm as he nodded eagerly just as it was obvious to Edwin that he had Alexander right where he wanted him.

Lord Malcolm Bruce, cousin to Prince Robert Bruce and Lord Mayor of Glasgow, was a man of enormous appetites. His bills for food and drink at the inn he had occupied for the last month were twice that of a normal man. And, Philip had reported that, according to his sources in the town of Roslin, he occupied the attention of two or three prostitutes a night. This was in addition to his much-younger wife, who spent most of her time keeping up with a brood of six children with another on the way.

Now, however, Malcolm did not look like the fun-loving epicure he usually appeared to be. He quietly stroked his beard, picking up a chunk of beef to pop in his mouth only occasionally as he explained in hushed tones the benefits Scotland could reap with Robert the Bruce at its head. It was quickly plain to Alexander that Malcolm was one of the best tools Robert had in his ongoing political war with Balliol and Longshanks.

"What, if I may be so bold to ask, young Lord, did my dear Stanton offer as incentive for supporting Balliol?" Malcolm's eyes were calculating as Alexander considered his trust for a moment.

St. Clair made his voice offhand as he replied, "Lands in the south, lower taxes and tithes, that sort of thing."

Malcolm grunted a chuckle. "Politics."

The younger man continued in the same tone. "And, of course, he guaranteed *prima nacta*."

Malcolm's eyes turned hard and his face reddened. He muttered something into his beard that sounded like "Bastard."

Alexander picked up a small hunk of beef from the plate between them and tossed it into his mouth, chewing slowly. He sipped at his goblet of wine as they looked at each other. "I have never needed the help getting women. Besides, I have a particular dislike of rape, even when it's prettied up with a fancy title."

Malcolm's grin was hard beneath his red beard as he sipped at his own wine. He chuckled again. "I've never been much of a fan of it myself, especially as it always seems to be the powerful granting it over the occupied. Which it seems we will be under Balliol."

"Then it seems to me that a wise Scottish leader would support the Bruce."

Now Malcolm's grin softened into a smile. "Seems that way, doesn't it?"

Alexander returned the smile. "Aye."

Sergeant Brian Kennedy hefted a sword and checked the time. Alexander was late. Brian looked over at one of the other Irish soldiers that had accompanied Alexander from Kincora. "Corporal," he called.

Corporal Mahon O'Dawson looked up from sharpening his blade. "Yes, Sergeant?"

Kennedy waved him over with his sword. "If Lord Alexander does not want his workout today, I still need mine."

"Lord Alexander does want his workout today, thank you, Sergeant."

"It is about damn time, my Lord."

Alexander slipped off his cloak and sword belt after he drew his weapon. He eyed Kennedy darkly. "Must I remind you of your manners again, Kennedy?"

Brian's smile was not pleasant to look at. "If you think you can, Sire."

With the last, he launched himself at the unguarded middle of his noble lord. At the last moment, Alexander spun out of the way, parrying the heavy slash with a strong sideswipe. St. Clair's blade swung quickly around in a high strike that was parried in turn by Brian's quick defense.

Alexander settled into a ready posture, his sword strong in front of him. "Now, I'm ready, Sergeant."

Brian chortled. "Good, Sire."

The two fenced back and forth for several minutes, blades dancing near exposed flesh before being blocked by the opponent's. Back slashes were parried by foreswings that carried back around to parries. It was a constant fight of attack, each man fighting for advantage. A low swing by Brian was met by a parry and Alexander's sword was knocked completely aside. Brian's sword was at the Earl's throat in a half-second.

Alexander nodded once to Brian and Brian lowered his blade. He chuckled at Alexander and walked back over to his gear. "Now that you are good and warmed up, my Lord, you can lead the men in their regular workout."

The Earl of Roslin sighed as he slid his own sword into its scabbard. It had been long practice between the two that whoever lost their warmup match would lead the men through their exercises. Alex turned to the others and chuckled. "All right, you dogs, on your feet."

The six other men who had come with him from Kincora rose to their feet slowly. They were all grinning. It had been a couple of weeks since Alexander had lost, a long streak for their regular contest. Alex stripped off his tunic and padded mail, baring his chest before the men. They all copied him, except Brian, who leaned against their wagon. "Ten-HUT!"

In a split second, all grins were gone from the men and their backs were ramrod-straight. As he started calling the cadence, the men went through a regular calisthenics routine, stretching the muscles they would need to work. As they finished, a fine sheen of sweat on their bare chests and backs, he turned and started at a trot. He led them outside the walls and picked up the pace.

Brian watched them intently. He knew they were at a razor's edge. Lord Alexander's fight the previous day with the three brigands had proven that. Brian knew that any of the men would be capable of defeating them, but not with such ease. He grinned distantly as he remembered the first time he had met the new Earl of Roslin.

Brian Kennedy was summoned into the great hall of Kincora. He had only arrived the week before and had only met the Lord of Kincora for a few brief minutes. He knew he had come highly recommended by the Earl of Armagh in Ulster. Brian's family had been in the service of the Hy Neill Clan for generations. Rumor had it that his father had been on the verge of being honored by a knighthood when he met his death at the hands of a pack of bandits outside Derry.

Brian had been raised on his family's heritage and his father's death. He had been trained by the best swordsmen that money could buy. He knew the value of conditioning and teamwork in battle. That was knowledge that Lord Michael O'Brian knew would eventually be valuable in the training of his squire, but first he had to learn how to handle himself properly. That would be Brian's first assignment for his new lord.

Brian strode forward, shoulders square and proud. He was young, but had already earned the look of a veteran warrior. He stopped before Michael's chair and lowered himself to his left knee. "My Lord," he said, his voice quiet but proud.

Michael studied his thick neck and strong back. Brian was a veteran of over twenty separate engagements in Ireland, Wales, and France. He had only been back in his home country for six weeks. He noticed a small scar on the back of the Ulstermen's left ear and wondered where it came from. He sighed softly and ordered Brian to rise.

Brian did and Michael stood to speak to him. "Sergeant Kennedy, I want you to take personal responsibility for training my squire Alexander in hand-to-hand combat. Teach him how to fight with his hands, his sword, and his wits."

Brian looked somewhat dismayed. "My Lord, he is but a boy who has no knowledge of fighting."

"I know. And the best teacher is experience."

Brian still looked somewhat confused. "But his experience will teach him only defeat at my hands."

"For now, you are right. But he will learn the hard way, if nothing else. Beat him, then teach him. Eventually, he will be good enough to hold his own against you, if not outright defeat you." Michael's smile was supremely confident.

Brian now looked skeptical. He had known plenty of nobles who had no ability to defeat him. Michael stepped up and clapped him on the shoulder. "Trust me."

Alexander looked up as Brian Kennedy approached him. The man was bare-chested and armed with only a sword. He did not look happy as he approached the Scottish lad.

"Pick up your blade, boy." Brian's voice dripped hatred.

Alexander gingerly lifted his sword and stood to face the Irishman. With a quick swing, Brian knocked the sword out of Alexander's hand and backswung his sword to slap Alexander on the leg with the flat of his blade.

Alexander shouted and rubbed at the red mark on his leg.

"Pick it up and hold it like a man."

Alexander was now mad and picked up his sword, holding it too tightly. He swung his sword at the man, who laughed as he whipped his blade in a circle and disarmed Alexander again. This time, the whip was across his forearm.

For the next hour, Brian made Alexander lift the blade again and again and continued to disarm him, making him pay for each drop with a stinging slash with the flat of his sword. Welts crossed his bare arms and legs by the time Brian was done.

"We will continue tomorrow, boy." Brian continued to talk to Alexander with the deepest contempt.

As the Irishman walked away, Alexander turned and ran into the great hall at Kincora, finding Lord Michael in his great hall, where he was deep in discussion on tax matters with his seneschal. "Lord Michael," shouted Alexander.

Michael looked over at him then turned back to his seneschal. "Just a moment, Rene." He turned away from the seneschal and faced Alexander. "Looks like you have had a rough afternoon, Alex."

The Scottish boy nodded eagerly. "An Irish soldier insulted and challenged me. He kept knocking my sword away and then he walked away like I was nothing and told me he would be back tomorrow."

Michael nodded slowly. "That was Sergeant Brian Kennedy. When he is done teaching you fighting skills, I will teach you strategy. Until you can fight, you are nothing in battle, and nothing to me. When you can hold your own sword, you might be worth something. Never interrupt me again."

With that, Michael turned his back on Alexander and returned to his conversation with Rene.

Tears stung the boy's eyes as he backed away from the Irish knight.

Brian looked up from his reverie as the six Irishman followed Alexander through the gate. The Scottish lad had grown into a powerful man who had few equals anywhere with a sword, or his bare hands. Day by day, his skills had grown until he could hold his own against Brian. The Ulsterman would never forget the first time that Alexander had beaten him. Through the quiet anger on his face, Brian had felt a powerful pride in the youth. He had stood at Lord Michael's side as the boy learned how to place and direct his forces, how to play chess, how to read and speak Latin and French as a gentleman should, how to dine in polite company. He watched the boy grow up into a man and now took pride in taking orders from him.

Alexander stopped in front of him and looked Brian in the eye. "Have you reviewed my troops?"

Brian nodded. "They look well-trained, but not as well as they could be."

Alexander looked around. "I am not surprised. My father was no mean warrior himself. And he was a strong leader of men."

"Aye, Lord. That he was." Brian was well-acquainted with the story of Sir Edward St. Clair.

"Tomorrow, I will review them with you and you can show the local Sergeants and Corporals their new training regimen. I want these men to be the best troops in Scotland."

Brian nodded again. "They will be, Lord Alexander."

Chapter 9

The train of riders that preceded the titular King of Scotland was impressive indeed. Twenty men in full regalia as lords of the realm rode in front of the carriage that carried John Balliol. Lord Alexander Mac Edward St. Clair, Earl of Roslin, stood at attention as the retinue rode into the gate. He lowered himself to one knee as the carriage door opened and King John Balliol stepped out.

Balliol appeared impressive enough. He was a large, barrel-chested man with a crown of thick silver hair. He wore a thick tunic crossed by a plaid of his clan and a thick gold band encircled his head. Unlike most of the men around him, who wore kilts and heavy riding boots, he wore pants and thin slippers. A stole of purple velvet was worn across his shoulders. He extended the end of the stole to Alexander, who kissed its hem.

"Rise, Lord Alexander," his voice came deep from his chest.

Alexander stood and dipped his head in salute. "Your Majesty," he said, loudly and clearly. Many of the men who traveled with Balliol nodded their approval of the young Earl.

"Do you wish to see your rooms, Majesty?"

The King of Scotland dipped his own head. "That would be well, my boy."

Alexander waved his arm into a bow toward Philip. "My seneschal Philip will conduct you to your quarters. My other retainers are available to see to your retinue."

"Very good, Alexander. I am well impressed by your hospitality."

"Thank you, Majesty."

Lord Alexander sat across from his seneschal. "I know the current state of Scottish royal politics, Philip. How did they get this way?"

Philip sipped from a goblet of wine. His staff was helping King John Balliol's staff get settled in to their quarters before dinner.

"Well, Sire, you know that when you left, King Alexander III was strong, if aging. He died without leaving a son. This was three years after you left for Ireland. That would make it 1286. A council was appointed to decide the next King. They decided to make Alexander's granddaughter, Margaret of Norway, the official heir. They would marry her to Longshanks' son Edward when she reached her majority, and they would rule Scotland together. But Margaret never made it to Scotland; she died along the way. That left them without a clear descendant, but that would not last long. Balliol emerged, as did John Comyn and Robert Bruce the Competitor, father of Robert Bruce the Earl of Carrick who is eternally absent, and grandfather of the Robert Bruce they currently push to the throne. Balliol has the most strength and the support of Longshanks. Rumor has it that Balliol's daughter is to be wed to the boy Edward. Hence, he is the King."

Alexander nodded, his head slightly spinning at the intricacies of Scottish royal politics. "What about Comyn and Bruce?"

"Comyn's not strong enough, and he never will be. Bruce has a large following among the nobles, but he wants to be independent of England and Longshanks. Therefore, Edward will not let him come to the throne so long as he has anything to say about it."

"He should not have anything to say about it at all. He has his own kingdom."

Philip smiled. "And he has the strongest army on the island, my Lord. None can stand against it."

Alexander sighed. "Maybe someday someone will be able to."

The door burst open and in ran Sergeant Brian Kennedy. "My Lord, men approach."

"Yes, Sergeant, men often approach Roslin." Alexander had never known Brian to show this kind of excitement.

"But, Lord Alexander, these men are Templars."

For the second time that day, Lord Alexander St. Clair strode out of the great hall to await a train of riders. He spotted this one as it passed through the gate of Roslin. There were more walkers than riders. Twenty men walked, clad in brown robes with simple ropes for belts.

These monks were escorted by four armed riders and their retainers. Each knight was clad in the white robes of the Order of the Temple. Their armor was worn under the robes and scarlet passion crosses decorated three of their white robes, both on the back and the left breast. Their helms were off and were carried, along with their lances, by a Sergeant. The Sergeants were clad in brown tunics decorated with the red passion crosses. A Templar chaplain accompanied the group, clad in a green robe and red cross. He walked while the other Templars rode.

A red patriarchal cross decorated the white robe of the leading Templar knight. He dismounted and bowed low to Alexander. Confusion clouded his face when he stood up straight. "Are you Sir Edward?"

Alexander felt Philip's eyes on him from the side. "No, Lord Templar. I am Lord Alexander Mac Edward St. Clair, Sir Edward's son."

The Templar nodded. "I am pleased to meet you, Lord Alexander. I am Sir Robert de Burghe, Preceptor of Edinburgh for the Order of the Temple. I and my Brothers are escorting these monks south to York and would greatly appreciate your father's aid in giving us a place to rest and refresh ourselves for the night."

Philip cleared his throat and started to respond. Alexander stopped him with a raised hand. "My apologies, Sir Robert, but you misunderstand. I am the Earl of Roslin. My father passed away recently."

Sir Robert crossed himself. "It is I who should apologize, Lord Alexander. I was unaware of your father's passing. He was a great friend to the Temple and I had spent many nights at Roslin in the last several years in his gracious hospitality."

"No apologies are necessary, Sir Robert. As you say, you were unaware. As to your men and charges, I believe we will have room for them." He turned to Philip and received a silent nod. Then he turned back to the Templars. "You have arrived at an opportune time. His Majesty, King John Balliol of Scotland is spending a few of his days with us and tomorrow, we will have a tournament in his honor. You and your men are welcome to participate."

Sir Robert smiled at the younger man. "We are honored to receive your hospitality, my Lord. It is obvious that your hospitality will honor us as your father's did. I place myself and my retinue in your charge. And I thank you deeply."

Alexander turned to Philip. "Philip, please afford these men places of honor at Roslin."

Robert turned and issued instructions to his men to look to the monks, horses, and equipment before seeing to their own comfort. His men nodded obedience with the air of men long used to following those orders. Before following Philip and the rest of his group away, he turned back to Alexander. "Lord Alexander, will you be taking part in tomorrow's tournament?"

Alexander stood a little taller as he answered. "Yes, Sir Robert. I will."

"Very good. With your permission, I will enter myself."

"I would be honored, Sir Robert."

Robert's smile was wide. "Then I will look for your shield in the lists."

Alexander's smile was equally wide. "And I will look forward to it."

Alexander stood naked on the balcony outside his bedroom and looked up at the stars. His new lover lay on the bed, snoring softly, satisfied by their lovemaking.

Suddenly, he was distracted by movement. The guard that stood outside the room shared by the Templars and their monkish charges was being relieved by one of his fellows. Alexander watched the military efficiency with which the report was made and nodded his silent approval. He watched as the relieved knight stepped silently into the room, silhouetted for a moment by the light that had to burn all night in Templar quarters.

New movement drew both the guard's and his attention. It came from the quarters afforded to the King. In fact, Alexander quickly realized, one of them was the King. The other was the Earl of Warrene. And it was the Earl who seemed to be giving commands to John Balliol. When Balliol refuted something Warrene told him, it was Warrene's voice that overrode Balliol's, something that did not sit well with the Earl of Roslin.

Warrene led Balliol back to his quarters and left the King there. He glanced around as though seeking watchers, causing Alexander to fade back into shadows. Warrene did not see the Scotsman and moved back to his own quarters. Alexander stepped back into his room and slipped on a robe.

He left his rooms and walked down the hall to Philip's quarters. He knocked quietly and waited patiently. He was greeted with the sight of Brigid, wearing a long tunic that hid her nudity from him. She dipped her head. "My Lord."

"Is Philip up?"

Philip opened the door wider. "Sire. Is there something I can do for you?"

"If you are not busy."

Philip looked down at Brigid and sent her back into the bedroom with a jerk of his head. She silently obeyed. Philip led his Earl into the sitting room and offered him some wine. Alexander shook his head, sitting down on a sofa. Philip sat across from him, sipping wine from his own goblet.

Alexander opened without preamble. "Why would the Earl of Warrene be giving orders to the King of Scotland?"

Philip considered it for a second. "Warrene is one of Longshanks' favorites. Rumor has it that, if Balliol is as weak as it is supposed, that Longshanks will rule Scotland through Warrene. Is Warrene giving orders to Balliol?"

Alexander nodded. "It certainly appeared that way."

"So, perhaps the rumors are true. If this information were to reach the ears of Robert Bruce, it could aid his cause with those nobles that are on the fence, so to speak. If, that is, you want English influence out of Scotland."

Alexander looked up and realized that Philip deeply wanted the influence of Longshanks out of his nation. "I very much want English influence out of Scotland, as do you."

Philip grinned a bit at Alexander. Alexander continued. "Can you get information regarding Warrene and Balliol apparently colluding to Bruce and his people?"

"Yes, my Lord."

"Then do it." Alexander glanced back at the bedroom door, where Brigid had cracked it open and was peering out at them. "In the morning, of course."

Philip smiled sheepishly. "Of course."

Chapter 10

The field was outside the walls of Roslin and had been cleared in the two weeks before King John Balliol's arrival. A grandstand with a special section for His Majesty had been built. King John sat in the center with the Earl of Warrene on his right. Earl Edwin Stanton sat on his left as his agent in Roslin. Alexander had been offered a seat in the presence of the King, but had forgone it to compete.

Now he waited, his horse, a fine white stallion named Bloodstone, properly outfitted for tournament fighting. His banner waited for his presence to be announced. He watched as the Templar Beauseant was placed across from the green and black banner of the Stuarts. Sir Robert de Burghe waited on the other end of the field while Sir Arthur Stuart was on the same end as Alexander.

Both men took lances and settled their shields in position. As the flag dropped, both men wheeled their horses and charged. They had already had to win three combats to get to this point in the final four jousters in the tournament. Now they rode hard toward each other. At the last instant, Sir Robert pushed his lance forward and raised the tip. His lance broke across the faceplate of Sir Arthur's helm. Sir Arthur dropped his lance and was driven from his horse. Sir Arthur landed hard but sat up and pulled off his helmet. A wry grin creased the Scotsman's face as the Templar turned his horse and rode back to his fallen foe. The French Templar removed his own helmet and extended his hand for a brace from Sir Arthur Stuart. A squire brought Sir Arthur's horse to his side and the Scotsman presented the reins to the Templar. Sir Robert took them and acknowledged the applause of the crowd before returning them to his opponent. It was a show of class that was more often repeated among men of power than not when they faced one another.

Alexander waved Sergeant Brian Kennedy forward and the Irishman brought the Earl's horse to his side. Alexander pulled himself up into the saddle and settled behind the leg armor. He took the helmet from another Irish sergeant and settled it on his head. He looked out through the slit as they took down the Stuart and Templar flags and put the banner of the McFarlanes on the opposite stand while the crenellated black cross on a white background that represented the St. Clairs was put on his end of the field.

Alexander closed his eyes for a moment and quelled the butterflies that were in his gut. When he opened them, it was not Sir John McFarlane that awaited him, just an opponent. He extended his hand and took the lance from Brian. The flag dropped and he spurred Bloodstone hard. The horses raced at each other as the lances came down. Alexander found the eyes of his opponent and saw a small bit of fear there. He drove his lance into Sir John's helmet, knocking him unconscious with the force of the blow, and unseating his fellow Scot.

The Earl of Roslin quickly unseated himself and ran back to the fallen man. After tugging off his own helmet, he drew a knife and cut the lacings that held McFarlane's helmet on before pulling it off. He felt around the other man's neck as others raced up.

"Relax, Lord Alexander," came the familiar voice of Sir Robert. "Let me see him."

The Scottish noble backed off as the Templar took over. His experienced hands moved quickly and efficiently. He lifted the Scot's eyelids and gazed at his rolled-up eyes. "It will be all right, everyone." He looked up and located Brian Kennedy by eye. "Do you know where there is vinegar?"

"Yes, Lord Templar."

"Good. Bring me some quickly."

Kennedy ran off quickly. Robert looked back down at his charge. "I think he is just concussed. Hopefully the vinegar will bring him around."

Alexander was very concerned. "I did not mean to hurt him."

Robert's eyes were full of compassion as he looked back up at Alexander. His voice was soft. "I know, son. These things happen sometimes."

The two men were interrupted by the Earl of Warrene. Alexander did not like his haughtiness. "His Majesty wishes to know when the tournament will continue."

Roslin and the Templar exchanged glances. Sir Robert spoke first. "Please inform His Majesty that the tournament will conclude in the morning when Lord Alexander and I will meet one another."

Warrene sniffed. "Can we not conclude it today? McFarlane can be dragged off to the side and the two of you can compete."

Now Sir Robert's voice betrayed annoyance. "We will first see to Sir John and his wounds. It could be dangerous to move him yet. When I am satisfied that it is safe to move him, we will move him. Until then, we will not. And if His Majesty has cause to argue with that, he can take it up with the Scottish Master." While he spoke, his eyes never left the face of Sir John McFarlane.

As Warrene stalked off, Brian Kennedy reappeared with a jar of vinegar. "Will this be enough, my Lord?"

Robert jerked his head in the affirmative. "It should be more than enough, Brian. You have done well." The Templar dipped his fingers into the vinegar and waved them close under the nostrils of the fallen McFarlane.

McFarlane's nostrils twitched and his eyes jerked open. "Where am I?" the fallen man asked, his voice full of alarm.

"Relax, Sir John. You had a bad fall. How do you feel?"

McFarlane looked up at the Templar. "My head hurts."

"Can you move your hands and feet?"

With an effort, the Scotsman did so. Robert then pulled him up and onto his feet. Sir John was wobbly, but could stand with assistance. He was led away by his retainers to the applause of the crowd. The two finalists stood and looked over at the grandstand, where John Balliol's crew had already departed.

Sir Robert snorted in disapproval. "So, in the morning?"

"If you wish it, Sir Robert."

Robert laughed. "Should I be worried, Lord Alexander?"

Alexander looked meaningfully toward Sir John McFarlane's departing form.

Robert followed his look and laughed again. "I am a combat veteran, Alexander, just like you. We are both already dead and living on borrowed time."

Alexander jerked his glance to his friend and chuckled back. "So we are. In the morning, then."

The two men exchanged bracing grips and waved to the crowd before departing for their quarters.

Alexander laid in Fiona's arms and listened to her deep breaths. Unable to sleep, Sir Robert's words echoed through his mind. "We are both already dead and living on borrowed time," he had said. They reminded Alexander St. Clair of another morning, before a battle.

The sixteen-year-old squire woke easily, more alert than usual as the Sergeants in the tent rolled out of their blankets and left to find tea and alert the men under their various commands. Alexander stood and stretched as Brian did the same. They both left the tent and went to the one next door, where Lord Michael O'Brian stood over a table that showed the latest dispositions of the army from Connacht. Figures depicting the combined army of Munster and Meath stood arrayed against it. Michael was deep in thought as the commander of his cavalry waited patiently.

Michael leaned over the table and began to speak. "Sitric, I want you to you're your cavalry in reserve and prepare it to support the main thrust of our army. That is where Connacht will mass their strength and there they will most likely outnumber us." Sir Sitric O'Connor bore the marks of a Nordic heritage in addition to the name. His stark-blond hair was almost white and flowed past his broad shoulders. He was from Dublin but very much respected the strategic mind of the Lord of Kincora. He silently nodded in response to Michael's command.

Michael continued, turning his attention to the larger man on his left. "Thomas, bring your men around our left flank to strike at their archers in the rear. Our pikemen should be able to hold off their heavy horse until you can scatter the archers and wheel around to strike them from the rear. Our right and left flanks will curl in behind you and seal off their center. Then Sitric will support our middle. We should tidy them up nicely." Sir Thomas McShane was a hulking figure who rode an equally-hulking stallion. It had to be to hold his weight. Still, he was an almost-legendary fighter in Ireland whose deeds were known all over the continent.

With these instructions in hand, the group broke up to give last-minute instructions to their men. Padraig would carry the instructions for Lord Michael while he prepared himself for battle.

Alexander knew his role and started to lay out the final acoutrements to Michael's outfit. It was his first time in battle.

"Are you scared, Alexander?" Michael's voice had a hint of laughter in it and Alexander colored.

"No, sir," the boy replied quietly.

He looked up to see Michael's smile. "You are either a liar or a fool. And I do not think you a fool."

Alexander realized that Michael's laugh had been a shared one, not one of superiority. He felt more ashamed than he had before. "Maybe I am scared, a little."

"It is right to be scared. I have been in many a battle, many alongside your father, and I am still scared, frightened about out of my wits. But, I have a good bunch watching my back. I trust Padraig and Brian. And I trust you to keep me alive."

Alexander's heart filled with what he realized was joy. He wanted to thank Michael for that trust.

But Michael was not done. "And you can trust me to do the same."

The pride that Alexander felt caused his eyes to water a little. "I will, my Lord."

Michael's smile was now a little sad. "I know. After today, lad, you will be like the rest of us, a veteran of combat. And, like the rest of us, you will be living on borrowed time. Because all of us that have fought really should be dead."

Alexander remembered little about the actual battle, except the fear. Parts of the fighting stretched into eternity while others flew by too fast to remember. He remembered the rain of arrows and bringing up his shield, trying to hide his whole body behind it. He remembered the thud of an arrow piercing right through it. He would always see in his mind's eye the Connachtman who had broken through to attack Michael's back and remember the feel of his sword cutting through the man's throat, the feel of hot blood spraying his face and stinging his eyes.

He would also forever remember the pride as Michael had turned and seen him cut the attacker down and the feel of a slap on the shoulder from his teacher. More, he would forever remember the night afterward, when Michael had sent one of the whores that followed the army into his tent to take his virginity. He had stumbled through the act, but his earnest efforts had won him a second go which was far more satisfactory.

Most of all, he would remember the next morning, when the serious knights had come to him and put him on a horse to lead him to a nearby stronghold. There, he was bathed and dressed and put on his knees to pray in the chapel. After what seemed like hours, he was led into the great hall of the building and made to kneel. There he swore oaths that he would always serve God and the Church, his king and country, but most of all the honor of knighthood. With his sword, Lord Michael struck a blow on his left shoulder and he was raised to his feet as Sir Alexander, a real combat veteran and knight.

A banquet was served after the consecration and Sir Alexander was given the honor of sitting on Lord Michael's right. Alexander noticed the strangely-dressed knights across the room, with their white tunics and red crosses. They seemed to stay out of much of the conversation and kept mostly to themselves. They carried themselves with a certain air of superiority that Alexander's young senses responded to.

"Who are they?" he asked his lord.

"Those are Knights of the Temple. They are better known as Templars. They serve God and Holy Mother Church."

"Do they not like to revel with the men?"

"It is forbidden to them to celebrate too conspicuously."

"Then why are they here?"

"They saw you in combat yesterday and were quite impressed. In fact, it was at their recommendation that it was taken up by us to go ahead and knight you."

"Why did they not fight alongside our forces?"

Michael laughed. "They are warriors dedicated to Christ. They are not allowed to take sides in secular disputes. So, they merely observed."

It was the first, but not the last, time that Alexander would be deeply impressed with Knights Templar.

Chapter 11

Lord Alexander St. Clair had now ruled Roslin for nearly three years. While little had changed in his little corner of Scotland over those years, affairs in other parts of the world were not revolving quite so smoothly.

Edward Longshanks continued to consolidate his power in England and his influence over Scotland. King John Balliol had defied Longshanks and been driven from his throne to be replaced by the Earl of Warrene, who Longshanks refused to allow to wear the crown. The English king's continued incursions into Scottish politics drove more nobles into the camps of Bruce and Comyn.

Meanwhile, stories had been spreading from the low highlands of a brilliant rebel named William Wallace, who defied the military might of England. It was unclear, however, whether Wallace supported Bruce, Comyn, or wanted to rule himself.

As tales of Wallace's rebellion grew and his legend was fed, Longshanks encouraged his English lords to claim greater control over their Scottish holdings. One of those lords was Sir Edward St. Clair-Taggart, who controlled the lands of the Taggarts around London in addition to the lands of his father in southern England and held the title Earl of Clarence. He also, under English law, was entitled to his father's lands at Roslin as the eldest son of Sir Edward St. Clair by his first wife, the Lady Eleanor Taggart.

Sir Edward was a mirror of his father but had no love for the backwards Scottish nation. He was, however, a close follower of his king. In 1295, he sent agents north to explore Roslin and, in 1296, he set out to claim the lands of his father from his younger half-brother Alexander.

Fiona laid back on the bed, her stomach rumbling with sickness. She patted her swollen belly and found herself laughing. "I get it, little one. You do not like spicy foods."

Five months into her pregnancy, her first pregnancy, she hoped, she was enjoying the approach of her child's arrival. She closed her eyes and started to drift off, a smile on her lips.

She had been sleeping for just under an hour when she awoke to the sound of her lover striding into the room. Alexander stopped at the foot of their bed and gazed at his love's pregnant form. He circled to her side of the bed and sat down beside her, his eyes on her face. A finger traced the underside of her jaw and her lips twitched.

Next, his finger traced her collarbone and he leaned over to kiss her in the hollow of her throat. A soft sigh escaped her lips as his tongue lightly touched her there Alexander looked at Fiona's closed her eyes and let his finger slide along the slope of her left breast, circling the nipple that stiffened under his touch. When he captured the nipple with his lips and caressed it with his tongue, she moaned deep in her throat. He continued his treatment of her breast as his hand traced over her belly down between her legs.

His fingers pressed the moistening flesh and fondled her as she gasped with pleasure. She pushed him back as she pushed herself up and tried to look severely at him. "How could you try such things with me? I am going to be somebody's mother!"

"Aye!" he responded, "I remember."

She laughed at him. Then she kissed him, her tongue toying with his while his hand moved back to its previous position. Her hand snaked under his kilt and she found his stiff pole.

As Alexander let out his own moan of pleasure, he pulled away from his love. They gazed into each other's eyes, both slightly out of breath. Fiona's desire was nearing its peak and urgency had entered her voice. "If you would get out of these clothes, I could do something about this." She gently squeezed him.

Alexander stood and quickly stripped off his clothing. Fiona grabbed him and pulled him into as close an embrace as her belly would allow, locking her lips again to his. She pushed her lover onto his back across the bed and threw one leg over his lap, straddling him and drawing him into her depths. As she settled onto him, she sighed at the feeling of satisfied fullness it gave her. She leaned over him and began to slowly ride him. The pleasure they both felt rose as their pace increased and Alexander slid his thumb under her to massage her clitoris. Fiona groaned and nearly collapsed as her pleasure increased exponentially.

She felt him contract and release his seed into her and shivered as the waves of her orgasm crashed onto the shores of her awareness. She bent down to kiss him and smiled as his arms embraced her. She felt his closing spasms and he slid out of her. She rolled off of him and he rolled onto his own side, pressing his chest against her back with his arms still tight around her. Fiona sighed contentedly and squirmed her bottom against her man. She felt his now-soft manhood nestled against her and smiled. Fiona closed her eyes and moved Alexander's hand onto her swollen stomach. He pressed his lips to her shoulder before laying his head down.

When Fiona's breathing deepened into sleep, Alexander extricated himself and stood. He stretched as he looked down at Fiona and smiled as he covered her pregnant body with a blanket. She clutched the blanket in her sleep, puling it around her. The Earl of Roslin leaned down and kissed his concubine softly above her left eyebrow, wishing for the millionth time that she would consent to marry him.

Alexander picked his clothes up from the floor and dressed. He stepped into the outer room to find Irina sitting on a sofa. He closed the door so as not to wake Fiona and joined his mother.

"Good morning, dear," she opened.

"Good morning, mother," Alexander replied, leaning down to brush his lips against her cheek.

Irina looked meaningfully at the inner door. "Is my chief lady-in-waiting up and about?"

Her son reddened slightly. "She was."

Irina laughed at his discomfort. "You are a randy pup, my son, just like your father. I remember him when I was pregnant with you. He could not keep his hands off me. Not that he was ever very good at that."

Despite his mother's apparent joy at the memory, Alexander was a little uncomfortable discussing his parent's sex life. His color deepened and his mother took even greater delight at this. She eased up on his feelings, however. "How is my grandchild doing, Alex?"

His color returning to normal, a simple smile broke Alexander's features. "He grows bigger every day, mother. It is hard to believe that he will be born in just four more months." Irina was pleased at his excitement.

"And his mother?"

Alexander's eyes sharpened, then softened. He knew that Fiona's refusal to marry him was partly a product of his mother's desire to see him marry and ally himself with a powerful family. Still, he knew that she cared deeply about Fiona and had selected his lover for a position of great trust.

"She is well. If you require her, I will wake her."

She shook her head. "No, Alex, I do not require her services at this time." She was saddened at Alexander's continued displeasure with her, but she felt that a dynastic alliance could lead her grandchildren to thrones and positions of power. She also understood Alexander's and Fiona's feelings for each other.

The uncomfortable moment between mother and son passed as a knock sounded on the outer door. Philip opened the door and stepped in. The seneschal's hair had grayed over the previous three years and his belly now stuck out over his belt. He had married Brigid shortly after Alexander had returned and his wife was shortly to give birth to their second child.

Philip dipped his head. "I am sorry to interrupt, my Lord, but there is a matter requiring your attention."

Alexander stood and scooped up his sword, girding it around his waist. Irina also stood. "I will check on Fiona, my Lord."

Alexander nodded once and followed Philip out at the quick step.

The scene that greeted the Earl of Roslin featured three of the dirtiest horsemen he had ever seen. They were accompanied by the Templar Robert de Burghe. Sir Robert bowed to Lord Alexander. "My Lord Roslin," the Templar murmured.

Alexander nodded by way of response. "How may we assist you, Lord Templar?"

The Scotsman could tell that the French Templar did not want to intrude on the liberties of long-time friendship but knew that only an issue of great importance would bring him to the gates of Roslin.

The Templar leaned close to Alexander and spoke quietly. "These men were separated from their company and need a secure place for a time. Warrene's men are looking for them."

Alexander eyed the horsemen, unable to hide a look of distaste at their state. "Exactly whose company are they a part of, Robert?"

Burghe's eyes looked as if he wished Alexander had not asked that question. He sighed. "Wallace's."

The Earl of Roslin's spine straightened at the name of the increasingly infamous bandit whose growing popularity was a thorn in the side of Longshank's power. And Alexander had no love for their English overlord or his puppet. He stepped away from the Templar and caught sight of the senior member of his military council.

"Sergeant Kennedy!" he called.

Brian Kennedy hurried over to Alexander's side. He saluted his lord and Sir Robert.

"Sergeant, clean these men up and outfit them in the kit of our Irish Cavalry. If any soldier of King Edward or the Earl of Warrene asks, we had them brought down from the highlands two months ago."

Kennedy dipped his head. "At your order, Sire." He hurried off to fulfill his charge.

Robert smiled at the Earl of Roslin. "I thank you, Alex, and the Temple will not forget this service."

Alexander chuckled. "They never do, my friend."

Over the intervening years, the Earl of Roslin had spent many a night in the hospitable arms of the Temple, and he never hesitated to return the favor by granting the warmth of his own hearth to a passing Brother. Sir Robert, who continued to serve as the Preceptor of Edinburgh, had spent several nights in the halls of Roslin, sharing his chamber with a Brother Templar while a lone candle burned in the room.

Alexander sat down at the head of the long table, his lover to his right. Sir Robert sat at his left hand, a retinue of three Templar knights having accompanied him for the evening meal at Roslin.

The blessing on the meal having been said, the company set out to demolish it. The Templars sat to the left of their Preceptor and ate in silence, except for Sir Robert himself, who kept up a lively conversation with the residents of Roslin. The Templar never had been able to keep his attention away from the beauty of Irina, who sat to Fiona's right.

Having noticed their glances before, Alexander would have entertained ideas of an affair between his mother and the Templar, but he also knew his friend's dedication to his vows. Still, he saw nothing wrong with them being friends, and he had made sure that they were both aware of that.

To Irina's right sat Brigid, her other lady-in-waiting, then Philip. Sergeant Brian Kennedy had seen to his soldier's repast, including his three newest, and now stood beside the door, to protect the sanctity of the meal.

All at the table were in high spirits when a quiet knock sounded near Brian's ear. Corporal Matthew O'Shannon appeared and spoke quietly to his commander.

"Sergeant, Sir James Newcastle is at the gate. He claims to represent the Earl of Warrene and demands an audience with Lord Alexander."

Kennedy nodded sharply. "Wait here."

He advanced quickly to the table and whispered the news to his Lord. Alexander also nodded. He wiped his hands on a napkin and stood to address the assembled.

"My deepest apologies to all, but it seems that a servant of the Earl of Warrene desires an audience. I shall return presently."

As he turned to depart, the silver-haired French Templar stood. "With your permission, my Lord, I will accompany you."

Alexander nodded and Sir Robert looked down at the man beside him. "Brother Lieutenant, you will remain here."

"Yes, Brother Preceptor." All present knew that an order received from a superior in the Temple was like an order from Almighty God.

The two men, leaving Sergeant Kennedy at his post, came face-to-face with Corporal O'Shannon, who stood at strict attention, his bright green eyes staring a hole in the wall opposite him.

Alexander and Robert silently approved as Alexander spoke. "Corporal, report."

"Sire, the Earl of Warrene's man asked us about any new arrivals. Feeling it outside our duty to make such reports, we refused. He then demanded an audience with your Lordship."

Alexander nodded as he exchanged a glance with Robert. Newcastle was well-known to both men as the one chosen to hunt down Wallace and his company. A veteran of the Crusades, he was not a man to be taken lightly.

"Present him in the great hall," commanded the Earl of Roslin. Corporal O'Shannon nodded sharply and trotted off to carry out the command.

The two veteran warriors exchanged glances and strode off.

Torches still burned brightly in Roslin's main hall, not yet being doused from the day's business. Alexander mounted the three steps to the dais along the eastern wall and took a moment to look at the chair that had been constructed by the local carpenter's guild for him. Several of his guests had commented that it rivaled the royal thrones at Edinburgh and London with its thick blue cushions and armrests.

His eyes rose to the stone walls of Roslin's hall. The masons' guild had employed masters from England and France to construct his father's dream. The tapestries that hid the bare stone showed pastoral scenes in deep greens and vivid blues. The Earl of Roslin turned and faced the white banner of the St. Clair family with the equiform, crenellated cross in the center. He breathed deeply as he heard the heavy tramp of booted feet intrude on his thoughts.

Sir James Newcastle strode in, still spattered with mud from the road. He was tall and thin, his lithe form displaying a power and grace that few men could dream of matching. The rattle of chain mail under his red tunic betrayed that he traveled prepared for action. His right hand rested on his sword belt while his helm was clutched tightly under his left arm, which ended abruptly in a black gauntlet that protected the wrist amputated by a saracen's sword on the plains outside Acre. The Duke of Leicester had left his hand there and cemented a legend for courage and toughness that was still repeated throughout the Christian courts of Europe.

Trailing the powerful strides of Newcastle were the shorter steps of O'Shannon.

The Duke of Leicester stopped at the foot of the dais and locked his black eyes with Alexander's blue ones. With an efficient move, he swept his hand to his brow and genuflected. His voice had a rich bass tone as he said, "Lord Alexander."

Newcastle rose and locked eyes again with the Earl of Roslin. In a lesser man, it would have been a brazen display of arrogance.

Alexander dipped his head in response, not breaking eye contact. "Sir James, I am honored to finally meet you. In what way can my simple office assist your august position?"

"As you are no doubt aware, my Lord, the Earl of Warrene has requested that I assist him by tracking the outlaw William Wallace. I had followed three of his men to your territory before I lost them. Have you intelligence on these brigands, my Lord?"

Alexander could feel Robert's glance. "No, Sir James, I have no information on any such men."

Sir James redirected his attention to Robert. "Lord Templar, have you heard of such men?"

Robert dipped his head. "As you are aware, Sir James, the Order may grant asylum to any it wishes."

Sir James voice dripped with venom. "Frankly, Lord Templar, there are regularly questions about those to whom the Order extends its friendship, especially in times such as these."

Robert's eyes smoldered. "Are you accusing the Temple of treason?" His hand snaked over his belly, ready to draw his sword at the wrong response.

Alexander cut off Sir James' sharp intake of breath quickly. "Sir Robert, I am sure that Sir James would suggest nothing of the kind." He turned back to the Englishman. "Sir James, there are no bandits at Roslin. We are loyal to our ruler and have no part in countenancing disloyalty or rebellion."

The two knights slowly relaxed as the tension ebbed. Alexander took a deep breath and, no longer believing the two would imminently come to blows, continued to speak to the Duke of Leicester.

"My Lord, can I offer you and your men refreshment? A substantial table has been set in my private dining hall. And there should be plenty for your troops as well."

Newcastle's eyes were still locked on the Templar's. He tore them away with some difficulty. "Thank you, Lord Alexander, but my men and I have our own provisions. I will return to my camp for the night. In the morning, by your leave, I will inspect your troops."

The Scotsman hesitated only for a moment. "Of course, Sir James, anything to stamp out treason."

The English knight nodded once before turning on his heel and stalking out of the room, once again trailed by O'Shannon.

When they were out of earshot, Robert's mocking tone rang in Alexander's ears. "'Anything to stamp out treason', Alex? 'We have no part in countenancing disloyalty and rebellion'?"

Alexander's look was equally exasperated. "And a simple 'No, Sir James, I have seen no one of that type' could not be said? I was trying to get him out of here. My records actually show the correct number of men in my army, and they do not show the three you brought this morning."

At that, Robert's smile was genuine. "Now you are worrying too much, old friend. Each of my Templars brought an extra robe and kit for just such an eventuality. When Sir James arrives in the morning, he will find the Preceptor of Scotland accompanied by six of his Brethren."

Chapter 12

Sir James Newcastle rode at the head of a column of mounted men thirty in number. They passed through the gate and Sir James reined in before Alexander St. Clair.

Brian Kennedy stood to Alexander's right, with Corporal Matthew O'Shannon on his right. Philip stood to Alexander's left. A handler from Newcastle's troupe ran up and took the reins as the Duke of Leicester dismounted.

Sir James sketched a salute which St. Clair returned. Alexander stepped forward to speak with him. "As you have requested on behalf of the Earl of Warrene and His Britannic Majesty King Edward Plantagenet, I present you with my troops. Their commander is Sergeant Brian Kennedy. My records are kept by my seneschal Philip Le Clair."

As their names were mentioned, each man nodded as indicated. James jerked his head to one of his men, who followed Philip to his office to review those records. While his man was tending to that, Newcastle inspected each of Alexander's Irish Cavalry and his larger infantry force, including the dozen axemen that were the spearhead of any attack he led. The Englishman was impressed at the toughness displayed by the Scotsman's troops. It was, without a doubt, the finest force he had seen assembled since watching the Templars and Hospitallers march into combat outside Acre.

When his assistant reported back that Philip's immaculate records jibed with what Newcastle had seen, it drew a terse nod from the Earl of Warrene's man. He turned and strode purposefully up to Alexander. "Thank you, my Lord, for your assistance."

With that, the English hero turned on his heel and stalked back to his horse.

As he pulled himself into the saddle, Sir Robert de Burghe led his men out of the stable. Alexander recognized the three knights he had dined with the night before and had to hide his shock at the appearance of the three brigands he had hidden the day before. They had been cleaned up but still had their thick beards, which helped them fit in with their "Brethren". The seven men in white Templar robes reined in their horses and the Preceptor dismounted and stroke to Alexander's side.

He sketched a bow. "My Lord, we thank you for your continued friendship and hospitality. We now take our leave of you and wish you a good day."

Alexander was used to such public formality and recognized its ultimate importance now. He responded with his own deep bow. "The Knights of the Temple are always welcome in my home, Lord Templar."

The two men shared a ritual embrace and Robert re-mounted his horse. He and his retinue rode out of the gate.

Newcastle had not deigned to pay great attention to the Templars' departure. He now looked away and ordered his own men's departure. Minutes later, Alexander ordered Sergeant Kennedy to dismiss the men to their regular duties.

His head splitting with a dull throb, the Earl of Roslin sought a cool compress and his dark bedroom.

Nearly three weeks passed before England intruded again on the affairs of Roslin.

In his role as noble lord, Alexander served to judge issues that arose among his people. This was a court day and Lord Alexander listened to an argument between two farmers who disagreed over the disposition of their father-in-law's cattle.

Alexander knew that many of his peers fobbed these particular duties off on their subordinates, but he truly enjoyed this role. He had heard the arguments and was prepared to render his decision.

Then the doors to the great hall opened and a ghost strode in.

Sir Edward St. Clair-Taggert was the very image of his father and held his father's title as Earl of Clarence. He had been promised a promotion in rank to Duke in exchange for taking control of Roslin. King Edward himself had promised it.

As the eyes of Alexander and his court studied Sir Edward, he studied these surroundings. He was actually impressed with their cleanliness. He had seen nothing but filth from the commoners in the countryside since leaving London. The only respite had been the city of York and, now, he had to admit to himself, this town of Roslin. It was obvious that, despite the poverty that reigned everywhere in Europe, the people, even those not noble, were well-fed. The great hall, where court was held, was full of people in well-turned-out dress. His eyes settled on his younger half-brother and he took the opportunity to study the man he was to turn out on his ear.

Alexander was obviously large and powerful in build. A relaxed grace was evident in his movements, rather like a lion at rest, but ready to strike at a moment's notice. His hair was thick and combined the rich qualities of being blond and red at the same time, the overall effect being a mane that women doubtless longed to run their fingers through. He was clean-shaven and his jaw was strong, displaying strength and beauty. For a moment, Edward regarded that this must be what Solomon had looked like, seated on his throne, rendering just and wise decisions.

The Englishman had to fight not to display the grotesque emotion that rose upon seeing his half-brother clad in a kilt. It was something he would never debase himself to do. His eyes saw the pregnant woman sitting near Alexander's left. He recognized that the man standing to his right, the light of recognition plain in his eyes, was no doubt a functionary. It was this fellow who came forward.

The two had never met, but it was obvious that the commoner must know who he was.

"Sir Edward." The statement mixed itself into a question. When Edward nodded, he continued. "I am Philip. I was seneschal to your father here and I continue to serve in that role for Lord Alexander."

Edward looked around. The sergeants and knights in the room must have realized what an older brother might mean to "Lord" Alexander's rule here, and they did not look pleased with the prospect. Circumspection, no doubt, would be the better part of valor.

Still, it would be better for them to start realizing his power. His voice was haughty but direct. "Have your master receive me in private. I have matters to discuss with him."

One of the sergeants, unable to hold himself back, stepped forward. "No man save the King may order Lord Alexander about." Edward could not miss the fact that the Irishman's hand had gone to the hilt of a sheathed dagger. And that was not the only weapon in the process of being reached for.

Edward's own hand settled on the buckle of his sword belt. He would not give in without a fight.

Alexander stood, drawing the attention of the room to himself to disarm their mood. His presence was breathtaking as he rose to his full height, fully six inches taller than his older half-brother. "It's alright, Sergeant Kennedy. Philip, escort Sir Edward to my private office. As for the rest of you, enjoy an early lunch. I will render my decision on this matter this afternoon."

With that, Alexander made his way to the floor and went to pass out of the hall. He heard the older man's whisper as he brushed past him. "Too bad they'll never hear your judgment."

Edward entered Alexander's private office behind the taller Scot and Philip the seneschal. The room was as grand as any other in Roslin with a table strewn with papers in the center. Alexander rounded the table and waved Edward to a chair. Edward sat and reached into his tunic, withdrawing a paper and passing it to the seneschal.

Philip read it slowly before passing it to Alexander. Alexander glanced at it. He had known about his father's first wife, about the older half-brother. He had worried as he became more known that this day might come. He still did not know what he would do about it.

"In case you can't read, my brother," began Edward, "that is a letter from His Royal Britannic Majesty King Edward Plantagenet. It orders you to vacate the office of Earl of Roslin and abandon these premises. It also orders that I am to take charge of these lands and people and bring them under proper English rule."

"You can't be serious!" This was from Philip, who looked thoroughly nonplussed. He also looked very angry.

Edward merely grinned coldly. "I am very serious, commoner. And don't interrupt me again."

Alexander stared coolly down at the top of the table and now looked up to his half-brother. "How can you do this to your family?"

"You are only family to me because my father desired to dally with a Scottish whore after my mother died. She gave birth to you, I assume under the bounds of a legal marriage, although who knows, with the unholy practices that pass in this land. Now, I have been ordered to leave my own home in London and travel to this backwater to serve this." His hand waved at the letter. "And now I'm supposed to run this territory. He actually expects me to stay here rather than return home." He shook his head. "I want no part of it, but I have no choice." This last was almost a spit.

Through his statement, Alexander displayed no emotion. Philip realized that he was angry, not only at the dismissal of Irina as a whore, but also at the other references to Scotland, a land that Alexander truly loved. He also realized, as others had learned too late, that Alexander did not need an overt display of emotion to be dangerous. As Edward watched, Alexander merely drew his dagger from its sheath and laid it on the table.

His voice was completely proper, but also completely cold. "There's no need to get personal, Sir Edward." His eyes bore in on his half-brother's. "And if you feel the need to further deride me, my family, my king, or my country, I will happily cut your heart out with that knife and have it placed on the highest rampart of this castle."

Edward stood rapidly, his hand on the hilt of his sword. Alexander moved similarly, picking up the dagger from the table. Edward was in a rage. "You may leave my castle as you wish, Sir Alexander!" He spat out the title like a curse.

Neither man suspected what would happen next.

Philip flew at the man, his own anger plain. Edward, his reflexes well-trained in combat, ducked low and impelled the seneschal at greater speed. He crashed to the floor, shaken a bit, but turned, the instincts of an assassin still strong in him. Edward's hands, however, had been busy. A small knife appeared in his hand and now flew across the room at the seneschal. It gleamed dully in the light, flashing once before burying itself in Philip's throat. Alexander knocked Edward down as he rushed to his chief aide's side. "Brian!" he cried, lifting Philip's body into his lap.

The Irish sergeant burst in and surveyed the scene. He drew his sword and advanced on the English knight, who drew his own sword. "No!" commanded Alexander. Only the years of discipline held Brian from the attack.

Brigid rushed in, coming to her husband's side. Edward pushed himself to his feet. His voice dripped with anger. "Alexander, this is how you treat a representative of the King of England. You will leave my castle before sunset. Or I will have you hanging from the highest wall by supper."

With that, Edward stalked out of the room, sheathing his sword. His eyes found Sergeant Brian Kennedy. "Sergeant, I will expect your troops ready for review at sunset."

Alexander's angry eyes followed his half-brother as his friend died in his arms.

Chapter 13

Alexander awoke, still unused to the surroundings of Fiona's old house. They had maintained it and even used it as a getaway spot over the years, but he never expected to live here. He shifted, feeling Fiona's comforting weight next to him. His left arm was around her, her head pillowed on his shoulder, her bottom against his hip. She mumbled in her sleep as he slipped out from under her. He leaned down and kissed her gently on the cheek. She smiled through her dreams. His passing had pulled the blanket from her full breasts and round belly. Alexander felt his manhood stir but covered her naked form with the blanket again.

The Scottish knight stretched, letting the blood flow freely to his muscles. He stepped out of the bedroom and into the main chamber of the small house.

His eyes took in the scene of the main room bathed in morning sunlight. He stepped out of the house, feeling the cold air on his naked skin and rounded the house to empty his bladder. He walked back around and slipped back into the house, to find Fiona, standing beside the bed and still wrapped in the blanket. She stretched her arms out to embrace her lover and they just stood there, holding each other for a minute.

Today, they would bury Philip. Alexander's grip tightened around Fiona's pregnant body, but not too much. He kissed her on the top of the head as he felt her tears run down his chest.

The priest intoned the benediction in Latin. Alexander stood at the priest's side, holding Brigid up. Fiona stood on the other side of her, holding her sister's hand. Anna stood behind them with her second husband, an intellectual nonentity who kept her bed warm and cared for her children since her first husband John had died, leaving her a very wealthy widow.

Despite the fact that Sir Edward had forbade his troops to attend the funeral, several had, chief among them Brian Kennedy and Ian McShane. They stood across the bier from Alexander. Their eyes met briefly and Alexander noted the anger that continued to simmer in Brian's eyes. He knew that it wasn't for him, but for his half-brother. A cold nod was exchanged between the long-time compatriots before they bowed their heads for the prayer, after which they were dismissed.

A band of pipers played a sad song. Bagpipes were good for that, even if they were illegal. The pipes were due to his longtime standing in the Roslin community, seneschal to two noble Earls of Roslin. And even though Philip had been English, his children, a son and one yet to be born, were definitely Scottish.

Fiona and Anna took their sister away. Alexander strode around the end of the grave as the men walked away, where he met up with Brian.

"My Lord," he was greeted by the sergeant.

"Sergeant," Alexander replied evenly.

The two strode away from Philip's grave in silence. It was Brian who broke it.

"I will not serve him, my Lord. If I must, I will kill him."

"Too dangerous. You would be an outlaw, hunted like Wallace."

"Perhaps Wallace's band would be a good hiding place for an outlaw. He needs good fighting men."

"I can not give you an order, even countenance an order, for you to kill my half-brother."

They stopped. "Alex, we can help Wallace. We can take out Edward and take refuge among Wallace's troops. You know they'll accept us."

"I can't, Brian. I have Fiona. With these wars coming, perhaps I will get an opportunity to have Roslin again. I pray that my days of fighting are over. I'm sorry, old friend."

Brian nodded, the gloom plain on his face. "Ian and I will leave the castle this evening. We are not the only ones. If you wish to join us, you are always welcome, my Lord."

Alexander nodded, his eyes finding the carriage that carried Fiona and her sisters. His horse was tied to the carriage. Fiona stood outside the carriage, waiting for him. He nodded again. "Thank you, Brian." The two men embraced as brothers.

The next morning found Alexander standing outside when a strangely-clad rider approached. His tunic and cloak were a dark yellow with black stripes. He wore trousers, unusual for the area, where most knights wore kilts of their clan tartan as Alexander wore. He rode up to the Scotsman and dismounted. The horse stayed firmly in place while the stranger looked around. Alexander gave him a guarded look as he waved before reaching up to remove his helm.

This revealed the silver hair and bearded features of Sir Robert de Burghe. The French knight bowed low as Alexander's jaw hung. His reaction gave the Templar a chuckle. "You look shocked to see me, Lord Alexander."

Alexander shook his head, grinning ruefully. "It is not your presence, but your appearance that is strange to me, *Sir* Robert."

This brought another chuckle to Robert's throat. "Sometimes, even those of us of the Temple must lay aside our proper dress to appear where we must. Now, get yourself presentable. I've come to bring you to a meeting."

"Meeting, eh? With whom?"

Robert laughed heartily. "Why, Master William Wallace, of course."

The Templar in non-Templar dress escorted the Scottish knight through the ranks of Wallace's band. He gave a short nod to two of the men he had helped so short a time before. For what it was worthy, he was still unsure as to whether or not he had done the right thing. He shook that off as the reins to his mount were taken and he dismounted.

Robert led him into a clearing. In that clearing was a man, who stood by himself, seemingly deep in thought. The man was huge, a good head-and-a-half taller than Alexander, with thick reddish hair and a matching beard. He wore a plain tunic and a kilt in the tartan of the Clan Stuart. Upon hearing their approach, he turned to face them. When he saw Robert, he grinned broadly.

"My Brother Templar." He bowed in fair imitation of any noble at court.

"How are you, William?" The two men braced their arms warmly.

"Fair, my friend." He turned his attention to Alexander. "And who is this?"

Robert waved Alexander over. "This is my friend and yours, Lord Alexander St. Clair, formerly the Earl of Roslin, driven from his seat by the interference of Longshanks upon the appearance of an older half-brother who just happens to have just been coroneted as Duke of Clarence."

Wallace's face showed a strong memory of the name. "This is the man who helped us with our lost sheep a few months back?"

"The same."

Wallace turned his full attention on Alexander. "I thank you for your help, Lord Alexander. If there is ever anything I can do for you or yours, please feel free to ask." His voice was full of meaning, which Alexander correctly translated.

He, however, still could not bring himself to ask for help in dealing with Edward. "I thank you, Master Wallace, but I can not ask you to harm my brother. He is, after all, family."

Robert's voice was quiet but strong. "Family who turned you out on your own, who murdered your seneschal before your eyes, who sides with a far-away king over his own and Scotland. That is the family you would protect."

Alexander found himself angry. "And family who, if I side with you and Master Wallace, I should be happy to destroy to further your cause. I want peace. I have a child soon to be born and I want my child to grow up without the constant fighting that has marked my youth and my father's life."

Wallace's voice sounded far-away when he spoke. "I wanted peace once, too, Lord Alexander." He reached out and gripped Alexander's arm in a brace. "My offer will remain open as long as I live, my Lord. God grant you peace." He turned his back on both men.

Robert now led Alexander away. But, Alexander knew that he had a new friend in the person of the great bandit of Scotland.

Thunder rolled loudly as Fiona screamed in pain. Alexander had sent Sean to find the midwife when she had woken up in labor. The knight did not know much about the process but knew enough about reading people to realize that the midwife was quite distressed. Fiona's water had broken an hour before and she was four months early for this.

Alexander's eyes sought God as he looked up to the ceiling, praying silently for her to be healthy, for their child to live well. Intellectually, he knew that the chances were not good for the first prayer and terrible for the second. He had hope nonetheless.

The midwife, her name was Tara, turned to the two men, talking to Sean. "Take him out of here."

Sean's rough hands guided Alexander out of the room. He took him to a chair, where the bigger man collapsed, his head falling into his hands. Myra, Sean's wife, looked sadly at the knight, knowing the sounds of healthy childbirth from her own experiences, and not hearing them from the bedroom. She looked out the window, staring at the rain and knowing that, whatever happened, there was trouble

The screams died in the next room and were not replaced by any other sound. Alexander's head came up, his cheeks streaked with tears. Tara opened the door and came to Alexander's side, kneeling down to deliver the bad news. Myra looked past the open door to see the form of Fiona. Her skin had always been pale, but now she was stark in the whiteness. The bundle next to her body was completely hidden from view. A roar of pain came from Alexander's mouth.

The funeral had been a small affair and now Alexander sat alone in the living room of the small house. The pain still cut through him, a dagger in his heart. Not just the loss of a lover and a child, but one he would always think of as his wife. Another tear dripped down his cheek, a well-worn path over the last few days.

His grief might only have been matched by his mother's. She had looked ready to sink into the grave with her former lady-in-waiting and grandchild. Anna and Brigid, both well-acquainted with grief, had stood up well, fully supportive of their sister's beloved.

The sunset had been lovely and Alexander had watched it, thinking it would have been one that Fiona would have loved. Now, stark night reigned outside. Alexander dozed in a chair, his chin resting on his chest. The knock startled him to wakefulness.

He rose and strode to the door, opening it warily.

The Templar Robert de Burghe, again dressed in his family clothing rather than his Temple robes, stood outside, accompanied by the large form of William Wallace. His voice was gentle. "Now, Alexander, are you ready?"

Chapter 14

The setting sun had broken through the clouds and burned down on the River Firth outside Stirling Castle. Wallace sat astride a huge stallion, gazing down upon Stirling Bridge. He grimaced at the man on his right, who studied the English camp on the far side of the river through a spy-glass and lowered it as a rider approached.

"Master Wallace," the rider began, sketching a bow from the saddle. "The English have over twice our number." A twinge of fear colored his voice.

Wallace nodded his thanks before turning to his fellow horseman. "Lord Alexander?"

Alex nodded absently, deep in thought. Finally, he turned his head to face the taller Wallace. "Warrene's strength would be in listening to Newcastle and men like him. But he places too much faith in Cressingham."

Wallace considered this. "What will they do?'

"I would ford the river upstream and protect the crossing from the high ground. It would make any attack by us too costly to be effective. Cressingham won't want to split their forces on hostile ground and will even argue that our strength is broken after Dunbar. He will want to keep his men close."

Wallace let his mind process the information. "So, they'll advance across and attempt to forge a bridgehead."

"Right," was Alexander's reply.

"And we attack and keep them from doing so."

"Wrong. Let them have the bridgehead and the confidence it will bring. Wait for the vanguard to cross, then attack frontally with your schiltrons while the cavalry flanks them from the high ground. They'll be cut off."

The light of admiration shone in Wallace's eyes as his leonine head nodded. "Can we sabotage the bridge so it will collapse at an opportune time?"

Alexander turned to the man on his right, who stood next to the big horse. "Sergeant?"

Brian Kennedy looked thoughtful, the shrewdness growing in his eyes. "I believe that can be arranged, Master William."

Wallace nodded. "Very good." He turned to address the other commanders. "Prepare your men to attack in the morning. We'll cut off the head of the English snake and free our land from the English. Meet in my tent in one hour."

Lord John de Warrene, Earl of Surrey, was regularly amazed at the appetites displayed by his fellow commander Hugh de Cressingham. Even as they made preparations for contact with the Scots, he munched on a huge beef rib. Apparently satisfied that he had gnawed off every edible chunk from the bone, he tossed it away and grabbed a wineskin from a nearby retainer. As he drank deeply, twin rivulets ran down his beard, staining his tunic as it ran down. He handed the wineskin back with a belch and dragged a fat, beringed hand across his mouth before reining in and rounding his horse to face Warrene.

Warrene took in the sight and felt a brief flicker of sympathy for the horse.

"I know those bastard Scots are waiting for us somewhere. That whoreson Wallace and his compatriots won't let an opportunity pass to strike at King Edward's standard."

Warrene merely sighed as he turned to face the implacable Sir James Newcastle. Newcastle's voice was cold. "Sir Hugh, Wallace is not all we have to worry about." He turned to address Warrene. "Sire, our agents report that Wallace not only has Sir Andrew Moray in his camp but has also been joined by Lord Alexander St. Clair."

Annoyance showed on Warrene's face. "Why couldn't Taggart deal with his damn half-brother when he had the chance?"

Cressingham burst into laughter. "Because the whole of Roslin would have come for him had he harmed one hair on Alex's head! Those people love Alexander and hate his brother. And in both cases, the feeling is mutual."

The Englishmen were interrupted by the approach of a tall, bearded Scot. Warrene glanced at Newcastle, a question in his eyes.

"Sire, may I present Sir Marmaduke Tweng. He joined us after Dunbar. He has proven a most effective agent since then." Tweng looked uncomfortable at the last sentence, but nodded a greeting to Warrene and Cressingham.

Warrene nodded back and greeted Tweng. "Sir Marmaduke, is there something we can do to be of service to so valuable a servant?"

Tweng still looked unsure of himself but responded well. "My Lord Earl of Surrey, My Lord Treasurer of Scotland, I wish you to know that I am familiar with this area. I offer to take a small force upriver and ford to protect the flank of your crossing from the high ground. I can take with me Sir Richard Lundie."

Suspicion darkened Cressingham's face. "And two Scotsmen can betray us to the forces of William Wallace, who no doubt will use his newfound cavalry to strike at our now-exposed flank. Sir Marmaduke, I am no fool and neither is Sir John de Warrene." He wheeled to face Warrene again. "I must protest at the mere suggestion of this renegade Scot. He has betrayed his own country and would now betray us to Wallace and St. Clair. We must keep our force together and not expose ourselves to unnecessary destruction."

Anger had long since darkened the face of Marmaduke Tweng. His dander up, he spoke angrily. "Sir Hugh, I find these remarks unacceptable and false. I have served faithfully under the standard of King Edward since the Battle of Dunbar and will serve it faithfully until this war has concluded. Even if that means following it to death."

Warrene held up his hand. "Both of you may cease speaking in the presence of your superior officer." He was more angry at Hugh than he could let on in the presence of the inferior Sir Marmaduke, no matter how much he agreed with the Scot. "Sir Hugh, Sir Marmaduke has served honorably and will not be spoken about in such an evil manner."

"My apologies, my Lord Warrene." Hugh's voice did not sound sorry, merely his words. "Still, I must insist that we keep our forces together. To split them would be unnecessarily dangerous."

"Very well, Sir Hugh, our forces will cross the bridge and forge a bridgehead on the opposite shore."

Sir Marmaduke dipped his head, still fuming at the insult offered by Cressingham. "If it please you, my Lord, I will bring up the rear of the vanguard."

Sir John de Warrene nodded, thanks evident in his eye. "Very good, Sir Marmaduke. Your valor will no doubt continue to be unquestioned."

Marmaduke nodded in return. "I should hope so, Sir John."

Lord Alexander stood at the head of the table, an arrow in his hand to serve as a pointer. On the table in the center of the tent was a map that showed the River Forth, the bridge crossing, and the known locations of the English encampment. Around the table stood Wallace, Sir Andrew Moray, Sergeant Brian Kennedy, and several others of Wallace's and Moray's troop commanders.

Alexander pointed to the Scottish end of the bridge. "We wait until they're bunched up just right at the end of the bridge, then Master Wallace and Sir Andrew will attack with the schiltrons and heavy infantry. Corporal O'Shannon will command them directly, but of course, he will be under your command. At dawn, I will lead our cavalry to this high ground." His arrow moved to the spot west of the road. "When the time is right, we will ride through and cut off the troops that are caught in the confusion, dividing the vanguard from the rest of the force." The arrow moved to a spot at the end of the bridge. "Sergeant Kennedy and his troops will prep tonight and wait here, under the bridge. When the cavalry rides through and divides the English, collapse the bridge. Let those men fall into the river, then come up and support the cavalry attack. We'll follow with the rest of the infantry to mop up behind the cavalry."

"What about our archers?" asked Moray.

"Good question, Sir Andrew," responded Alexander, nodding. "When our attack commences, have our archers fire over the river. That should make any support from their archers difficult, to say the least."

Moray nodded by way of response, impressed by Alexander's battle plan as he had been by his courage in the skirmishes they had fought over the preceding weeks. Lord Alexander was obviously a brave and intelligent fighter who knew how to use not only his personal abilities, but also the strengths of his men.

Alexander looked around for any more questions and found none. He deferred to Wallace.

The big Scot stepped up to the table and looked at the faces of the commanders of his army. His voice was gruff when he spoke. "My friends, word is already spread through camp about the size of the force we are facing. Tell your men that we have better weapons and better leaders. Overall, we have a better plan. Make sure they are aware of this. Only together can we hope to defeat our English opponents. If even one man runs, we might face disaster.

"Finally, I can not question your personal courage, but it must be on display tomorrow. Every one of you must offer personal battle against the English."

The big man's head bowed for a moment, then he looked up. "For Scotland!"

The others nodded as a man. "For Scotland!" they echoed.

Chapter 15

The dawn broke bright and clear and found the English force under Warrene and Cressingham mounted and ready to march. It also found Scottish woodsmen watching them from cover.

Michael Morgan was one of these woodsmen. His position across the River Firth afforded him a perfect view of the English forces. When the standard bearer of the English came across, followed by Hugh de Cressingham, he sent his son Joshua sprinting through the woods. He smiled before turning back to observe the English invaders, pleased that the boy's passage made as little sound as a light breeze.

Young Joshua made his way to the side of Sir Andrew de Moray, who would lead the Scottish infantry's left. He, in turn, sent runners to Wallace on the right and Lord Alexander in command of the cavalry. By the time Joshua returned to his father's side, a sizable contingent of the English cavalry had already crossed.

From their vantage point, the Morgans could see a small team of men using saws and other cutting tools to weaken the supports under Stirling Bridge, using the noise of the army's passage to cover the sounds of their sabotage.

A shout from the road drew Cressingham's attention. He had no idea what he beheld.

A pair of walls of long pikes faced him, advancing steadily. With a quick turn of his horse, he ordered his front ranks to attack the two strange formations. The double row of horsemen spurred their mounts forward, lances at the ready. The English knight could see their commanders mounted behind them and instinctively knew they had to be Moray and Wallace.

And in that moment, the Treasurer of Scotland recognized the value of the Scottish formation. He waved his sword, shouting and trying to call a retreat, but it was too late. The sharpened pikes struck the horses of the English cavalry. The schiltrons were Wallace's idea and gave dismounted infantry a weapon against mounted troops. As their horses died, the knights fell to the ground and were finished off by the swords and daggers of the ranks behind the pikes.

A stunned silence reigned on the English bridgehead. Cressingham broke the silence by waving to those on the bridge, calling them forward as fast as they could move. He was not bothered by the sound of hooves thundering from the side of his force.

With a strong charge, the Scottish cavalry rammed its head into the side of the English force. He wheeled in time to see the Scottish horse break through, led by the powerful armored form of the former Earl of Roslin. He had never had a real problem with Lord Alexander St. Clair, and really rather admired him, as his brother was nothing short of a real bastard. Those feelings he stuffed away, knowing that now he had to fight Alexander.

The Scottish cavalry cut off the advance of the reinforcements on the bridge, causing those men to bunch up on the narrow bridge. As the portly Englishman swung his sword at the advancing Scottish cavalry and noted the charge of the schiltrons, who were starting to break against the English cavalry that was attempting to separate from the newly-arrived enemy, he heard a strange cracking sound. He turned, tracking its source to the bridge itself. He focused on it just as the men trapped on it realized what the sound must mean.

Hugh de Cressingham watched their faces change to looks of pure horror as the bridge collapsed under them. They tumbled, armored men and horses, into the swift moving River Firth, which quickly swept them away. He recognized the man at the edge, an English warrior, no, a Scottish turncoat, Sir Marmaduke Tweng. Tweng circled his horse and fought to recover. His sword now swung at the back of one of his English compatriots. He continued this attack until it was obvious to all that he was not attacking out of confusion, but that he had turned back to his original side.

The large Englishman looked meaningfully across the river, seeking the support of archers he knew should be firing at any moment. He watched the bowmen fight their way to the front only to see the looks of horror as a rain of arrows fell from the Scottish-held side of the crevasse.

Cressingham cursed and sought the Scottish commander. He saw Lord Alexander, locked in combat with Sir Richard Lundie, another Scottish traitor. His eyes brightened as he fought his way toward the former Earl of Roslin, now an ally of William Wallace. Alexander caught the shadow of the larger man's presence and turned his head enough to catch him out of the corner of his eye. Hugh was pleased that Alexander would at least see his death coming.

Hugh never saw his own, as a dismounted Sergeant Brian Kennedy drove his own sword into the large Englishman's side, the blade ripping through chain mail and slicing through his heart. A hot spray of blood flashed over Kennedy, followed by Cressingham's own instinctive swing, which cut through flesh and bone and cut deep across Brian's collarbone. Kennedy's own blood coursed out, released by the Englishman's blade. Alexander shoved Lundie away and swung his sword across Cressingham's throat, finishing the job that his old friend had started.

As the English Treasurer tumbled from his saddle, falling to the ground, Alexander brought his sword back to stab into Lundie's chest. He watched the life fade from the traitor's eyes as he yanked his sword from the dead knight. Alexander St. Clair saw an unfamiliar knight now fighting three English knights. He rode swiftly to Sir Marmaduke Tweng's side, rescuing him by attacking the English warriors from behind. He helped the former Scottish turncoat dispatch those three before riding off to find more business.

Big William Wallace watched Andrew de Moray fall, cut down by two English knights. His huge claymore cut one of those knights cleanly in half, cut across the chest. As his arms, chest, shoulders, and head fell from the rest of his body, the legs continued to spur his horse on. The second knight had time to turn and try to escape, but Wallace's blade was faster. The big Scottish bandit threw his sword, impaling the second knight through the chest and destroying his lungs. Wallace rode over and leaned down to pull his sword from the fallen Englishman. A last breath of air escaped the body as he tugged his sword out.

As Michael and Joshua Morgan watched, the forces of Moray, Wallace, and St. Clair destroyed the English vanguard while the other Englishmen, on the opposite shore, had no choice but to watch the destruction of their army from afar. Wallace rode to the edge of the river, his forces victorious. He smiled broadly and waved grandly. "Warrene, send us some more!" he shouted, the bliss of victory plain in his voice.

From his vantage point across the river, Alexander, numb with the loss of his friend and marshal Brian Kennedy, watched Warrene silently fume.

William Wallace had spent the day in prayer. He had been bathed and dressed in a white tunic with a kilt in his own Stuart tartan. The great hall was filled to capacity with admirers of the brigand who would this day be given the greatest honor he could receive from the hands of his fellow warriors.

He was escorted in by several men, including Sir Marmaduke Tweng, who had been easily accepted into the fold of Scottish knighthood by the men. Tweng commanded the honor guard. He told Wallace to kneel. Alexander stepped forward.

"Master William Wallace," he intoned, "it has been requested of me to grant you the office and honor of Knighthood. I will be pleased to do so, but first, I must administer the proper vows. Will you be brave in the face of your enemies, a strict guardian of womanhood, and a pillar of Holy Mother Church?"

Wallace nodded once gravely. "I will."

Alexander's hand struck like lightning, the smack on Wallace's cheek echoing in the large room. "That is so you will never forget your oath."

Alexander drew his sword. He touched Wallace on the left shoulder. "In the name of God, St. Michael, and St. Andrew, I dub you a knight." He sheathed his blade and extended his right hand. "Arise, Sir William."

The handprint on his face slowly fading, William grinned and embraced Alexander in a bear hug. The assembled, most of whom were not noble, cheered raucously.

Lord Alexander and the newly-made Sir William Wallace were called away. Robert de Burghe escorted another man, whose face was hidden by the cloak and hood he wore. The two Scots accompanied the Templar into a room where they could have some privacy.

"What is this, Robert?" asked the former Earl of Roslin.

Robert waved at the new arrival. "This is Sir Robert the Bruce, the Earl of Carrick, and, I believe, rightful King of Scotland."

The Bruce removed his rain-soaked cloak and stood before Alexander and William. Neither had ever met the Bruce, but had heard many things, both from his agents and those of John Balliol, whose rule of Scotland was now questioned, at best.

He was young, but a fire burned in his eyes that both men recognized. It was a fire that both of them, and the Templar, possessed. It was the fire that men follow, into battle, even into death. They nodded their greetings to the young Earl of Carrick.

"Sir Robert," intoned the Templar Preceptor of Edinburgh, "this is Lord Alexander St. Clair, formerly Earl of Roslin, and Master William Wallace."

Alexander chuckled. "That's *Sir* William Wallace. He was knighted this evening."

Burghe's eyebrows lifted. "Truly? Well, congratulations, *Sir* William."

Wallace's eyes sparkled a little as he nodded his thanks. His voice was low and dangerous. "Why have you brought the Bruce to my presence, Lord Templar?"

Burghe was completely in control, but there was uncertainty in his look. "I thought it important that you meet, Sir William. I also thought it important that the Bruce and Lord Alexander become acquainted."

Wallace's timbre did not change. "This whoreson has continued to support the troops of Longshanks, even as we have struggled to find victories. His agents have continued to be just as traitorous to us as the agents of Balliol."

The Bruce's voice crackled a bit with youth. "Sir William, you must understand that I still have to honor my father's wishes. So, I have supported King Edward. I have waited for a strong victory to support you in your endeavors and yesterday was such a victory. I congratulate you on it, by the way, and your knighthood."

Alexander had remained silent, listening, and watched Wallace. He knew the big man's temper better than the others and was able to foresee what happened next. For William Wallace, though now a knight, still had the passions of a commoner and the ideas of a man who could get what he wanted mainly through force. And he had heard William rail against both Balliol and the Bruce. He watched the big man's hands flex, as though crushing something in his hands.

Alexander dashed between the two as Wallace came forward. Wallace's voice was powerful through clenched teeth even as his forward momentum was stopped. "You and Balliol have betrayed Scotland! Bastards like you killed my wife, took Alexander's land from him, and today, took Andrew de Mornay's life! Go back like the dog you are to beg scraps from Longshanks' table and, if you ever become a man, come back and challenge me for the soul of Scotland! Until then, stay out of my way!" Wallace turned away from the Bruce before his desire to strike the man grew any stronger. He stalked back into the other room.

Robert the Bruce looked stricken with betrayal. "Lord Alexander, does he speak for you?"

Alexander considered the young man for a few moments before answering. "Whether or not he speaks for me is not the issue. The issue is that he speaks for Scotland."

The former Earl of Roslin nodded to both men and strode toward the door. At the threshold he turned back. "If you want Sir William or me in the future, it is important that you support us now."

With that, he left the Earl of Carrick in silent contemplation.

Chapter 16

The rising sun after a night of rest did nothing to improve Alexander's mood. He still did not like the battle plan. He didn't know if he ever would like it.

But he did know that he was stuck with it.

He sat astride his stallion behind the line, where four schiltrons had formed below him. William Crawford rode back and forth between them, encouraging and giving last minute instructions. Marmaduke Tweng held his cavalry in check on the Scottish right. As at Stirling a year before, Wallace was mounted on a powerful steed. This occasioned a smile from the former Earl of Roslin, the first and last smile of the day, as he thought that only a huge horse could hold the knight from Elderslie. Wallace would stay behind the schiltrons and hope that the English left would leave itself as open to a cavalry charge from the flank as they had at Stirling. Again, Alex shook his head. You wouldn't get far planning on your enemy being stupid.

Alexander took a few moments to remember the nightmare raid on York, when it took a last-chance attack with something akin to Greek fire to turn the advantage to the Scottish army. Seeing the Duke of York dragged before Wallace, Alexander had strongly suggested mercy, a shout drowned out by Tweng's ardent talk of avenging the wrongs done by the English on the head of King Edward's nephew. Since then, Wallace had come to listen more to Tweng than he listened to Alexander. Now Tweng commanded the cavalry, a cavalry almost completely recruited since the Battle of Stirling. Very few had remained with the big man through the intervening year. The former Earl of Roslin shook his head again.

A spyglass brought the advancing English army into better focus. Alex prepared himself for the grim work as the schiltrons began to advance. Suddenly, the English left charged forward. For a few moments, a glimmer of hope awakened in Alexander's breast as he watched the English charge at the schiltron that screened the Scottish cavalry. He watched Tweng raise his sword and, at the precise moment of contact between the English and Scottish forces, lower it and order a retreat.

The Scottish cavalry calmly left the field. Alexander drew his own sword and charged down toward the fray as he heard Wallace's outraged cry. His first contact with the English brought his blade through the top of one English knight's skull, cleaving it across. The rider's body slipped to the ground as the horse continued toward the Scottish rear. Alexander didn't have time to study the phenomenon, however, as he continued his own advance. He didn't see the English right begin to consume the Scottish left. He didn't realize that King Edward simply sat back and watched, the heart of his army holding back until just the right moment.

The schiltrons had been split and the English cavalry rode hard through their remains. Scotsmen on foot were no match for the mounted English. Alexander waded through bloody fighters, his sword cutting a swath through the English cavalry and their follow-on infantry, searching for Wallace and Crawford. Crawford was on the ground, threatened by a mounted Templar.

A Templar?, cried Alexander's mind as he began his advance on the Holy Knight's unprotected left side. He wouldn't make it there in time, he knew. But he would have the opportunity to avenge Crawford's death. The Templar's sword fell, slicing through Crawford's neck.

Wallace's black charger came from nowhere and the huge Scottish warrior launched himself at the English Templar. Sir Brian Jay, Master of the Temple in England, was a close ally of King Edward and was only aware of a huge figure flying from his side. He turned to meet the new threat just in time to be knocked from his saddle. Jay raised his sword to strike at the bigger man. One huge fist struck the blade from his grasp. Another crashed down on his helm, stunning him. Wallace drove his blade into the throat of the Templar with one powerful thrust, instantly coated by the spray of blood from the severed jugular. He worked the blade back and forth, rich, red blood flowing over his hands. With a gurgle from his cut throat, the English Master died.

Marmaduke Tweng was still mounted as he rode up on Wallace's rear. Alexander struck at him, shocking him to awareness. Tweng barely parried the blow and struck on the backswing. The two mounted knights fenced as Wallace waved a Scottish warrior to his side.

"The fire!" Alexander heard Wallace say.

The kilted boy ran off, avoiding the continuing fighting in his mission. Alexander didn't have time to react as he continued to fight the turncoat. The two men finally came off of their horses but never missed a beat. Tweng brought his blade up high as St. Clair's knee buckled beneath him. The traitor's sword drew high and Alexander slid a dagger into his left. He struck under Tweng's ribcage, the blade skewering his heart. Somehow, Tweng held himself up, struggling to live despite the fact that his heart was now pumping blood into his chest cavity instead of arteries and out through the widening cut in his chest.

Alexander watched the life leave his eyes as his sword slipped from a nerveless grasp. He pulled the dagger out of the fallen man's body and cleaned the blade on his tunic. He slipped it away as he picked up his own sword and turned to face Wallace. The two men were an island of calm in the ocean of battle.

Wallace looked around. "Get out of it, Alex, while you still can. I sent a man to start the fire. Hopefully, His Majesty will get just as burned as the rest of the field."

Alexander nodded mutely and spotted his horse. He gathered in the steed and mounted as he saw the flames start. He knew they would spread quickly as the pitch had been spread all over the field, another last-chance effort. Alexander spurred his mount away from the field.

He didn't see his half-brother, who had lately joined the English army. Edward Taggart's blade came down toward his younger sibling's neck. The shadow from the spreading flame left his image burned into Alexander's mind as he turned his shoulder at the last moment. The blade clanged off his shoulder armor, cutting his tunic and splitting the mail. He could feel the sting of the steel even as he turned in the saddle, swinging his blade up at Edward. The Englishman parried the cut but didn't have a counterblow. So, the two circled on horseback before resuming their fight. Edward tried to force Alexander left, hoping to exploit the cut on his shoulder armor. Alexander simply held him off, looking for any opening, knowing Edward's impatience.

It finally paid off. Edward lunged to Alexander's left and the younger man simply backed his horse off a step. Off balance, Edward was an easy target as Alexander leaped from his charger, his sword clanging against the older man's armor. Red hate clouded the Scot's vision as he drove Edward to the ground. Both men's swords clanged to the ground as they landed. All Alexander could think of was Philip as he ripped the helm from Edward's head. He raised a fist and brought it down again and again on Edward's face. He could feel bone splinter under his blows as he struck. The Duke of Roslin died there on the fields at Falkirk at the hands of his younger brother. Alexander, mailed arms coated in Edward's blood, found himself off balance as he stood and the flames reached that area of the field. He tried to run but fell, landing atop Edward's body even as the field caught fire.

　　　The red engulfed the Scottish knight, even as he realized that he was again entitled to his home at Roslin.

Chapter 17

Lord Alexander St. Clair was alone.

He had ridden away from the fiery mess at Falkirk with burns on his back and arms. He had lost his sword somewhere in the mess. His horse had been shot out from under him in the escape. He had trudged here to this tavern in Edinburgh, hoping to make his way to the port to use what resources he had left to get to France. He shivered at the memory of watching William Crawford die from a Templar's blade. From what he had heard, Wallace himself had also escaped, but he had no idea how to contact the big Scot.

Alex had to fight to keep from jerking his head up when the two English soldiers came in. He watched them from the corner of his eye and fingered his knife, knowing that surprise would be his best weapon. They didn't even look at him as they selected seats nearer the fire and called for a wench, who came with drinks. The two Englishmen had to be able to feel the dark looks they were getting from the Scots around them. Still, they were loud and coarse, one of them popping the too-skinny barmaid on her thinly-covered bottom as she left them. They were too secure in their own power, knowing that any Scotsman who dared touch them would find himself hanging from the end of an English rope by dawn.

Alex knew an inn nearby that was friendly to Wallace's men. Hopefully, they would still be friendly to him. He got up and sidled quietly out the door, unnoticed by the boisterous Englishmen.

The street was dark and he kept to the darker shadows at the side. He didn't see the man in the darkness. A strong hand clamped over his mouth and he was pulled back through a doorway and into a small unlit room. He struggled but the other man had leverage. Then the voice spoke near his ear. It was a familiar voice.

"Relax, Lord Alexander. Relax. I'm a friend."

He stopped struggling and turned to face the voice while its bearer lit a candle. The small, flickering light came up to eye level and revealed the silver hair and bearded features of the Templar Robert de Burghe. Robert could see the distrust reflected in his friend's eye. And Alex couldn't hold his tongue.

"Friend? Your English Master was part of the retinue against us at Falkirk. I watched Wallace kill the man himself."

Robert sighed deeply. He had heard about the battle and knew this might be a problem. "Brother Brian did not have the support of the Grand Master. In fact, I doubt that Brother Jacques was even aware of it. When he hears, I doubt he will be pleased."

Alexander still looked distrustful, but gave a grudging nod. "You seem to have all of the answers, Lord Templar."

Another sigh from Robert. "Old friend, I came here to offer you help. Already your description is flowing from Falkirk. They want you, they want Wallace, they want any they can get from your band. If you request sanctuary, however, I can help you."

Alex nodded again, deciding to trust the French Templar a little more. "I do want sanctuary."

Robert blew out the candle. "Then follow me." The Templar looked both ways out of the building before exiting. They moved quietly in the shadows, down three different streets before coming to the door Robert was looking for.

The light was warm and inviting in the Templar Preceptory of Edinburgh. A guard came up immediately as Robert entered and saluted strictly when he recognized the Preceptor. Robert returned the salute and led Alex through the house and into a guest room. Alex was warmed to see clean clothing laid out and a basin of clean water, along with soap and washcloths waiting at a bedside table. Robert nodded over at the supplies and clean clothes. "Get cleaned up and dressed, my friend. Then come out and the guard will lead you to the Commander's quarters. We will talk more then."

Alex nodded and Robert left him alone. The former Earl of Roslin took off his torn and dirty clothes, stretching tired muscles and really wanting nothing more than a good night's rest. He took a washcloth and soap and began to clean the encrusted dirt and dried blood from his body. The water was thoroughly filthy by the time his body was clean. Alex pulled the tunic over his head, tightening it at his waist before wrapping the red-and-green tartan kilt around his waist, draping the remainder of the plaid over his shoulder. He tucked his dagger into the boots he pulled on and opened the door.

A brown-clad Templar sergeant stood outside his room and dipped a head in mute salute.

"Lead on, Sergeant," the Scottish lord commanded. The Templar led off and Alexander followed. The pair stopped at a door and the sergeant knocked solidly three times.

"Enter," came a Spanish-accented voice from inside.

Alexander could scarcely believe the sight that greeted him. Three white-clad Templar knights sat around a table with one empty chair. A swarthy Templar sat on Alexander's right side while Robert de Burghe occupied the seat on his left. The surprise was facing him.

Lord Michael O'Brian had changed very little over the intervening years. His face still seemed to be made of granite while thick, black hair continued to hang to his collar, even though it was now streaked with white. A similarly-specked beard covered his lower face, but the eyes were the same, still powerful, still bright. The Irishman stood slowly.

"Alex?" he asked, his voice scarcely a whisper.

"Sire?" responded the Scotsman.

Michael moved quickly around the table and threw his arms around the younger man in a strong embrace. Alexander squeezed back. He couldn't fight off the tears that flowed freely onto Michael's shoulder. He could feel a similar moisture on his own as the two old friends, teacher and student, knight and squire, father and son, grasped each other desperately.

It was several moments before they parted. Alexander looked over at the shocked look on Robert's face, not to mention the one he didn't know.

Robert stammered a bit before coming out with his prepared speech. "Lord Alexander, I would introduce you to Brother Michael O'Brian, the Master of Ireland, but it would seem you're already acquainted."

Alex dragged the back of his hand across his eyes. "Robert, Lord Michael was my master in my days as a squire. He and my father were the dearest of friends and I was sent to live with him and his wife Moira ... Sire, what about Moira?"

A sad smile creased the Irishman's features. "She passed over a few years ago. That prompted me to take the Vows of a Templar. I was sent immediately to Acre, where I was first blooded. Last year, Brother Jacques appointed me to return to Dublin and become the Master of Ireland."

Robert nodded, understanding easily the bond between the two men. He gestured to the swarthy Templar who had remained seated at the table, looking crossly at the three of them. "And this is Brother Jaime de la Cruz, Commander in Edinburgh. These are his quarters, and this is his Preceptory."

Alex nodded at the seated Commander. "Worshipful Brother Jaime, I thank you in advance for your hospitality."

The Spaniard suppressed a snort and nodded. "Do not thank me, Lord Alexander. Were it not for the orders I received from the Brother Preceptor, I would throw you out on your rebellious ass." He jerked his head. "But Brother Robert's orders were different. So you are here." Now he stood, looking up at the other three men from his somewhat diminutive height. "Now, if you will excuse me, I have a Preceptory to run and I would like my rest. Brother William will show you to your lodgings."

The three men left the Commander's rooms and followed the sergeant past the common room where the rest of the Templars not on duty were already asleep. The room assigned to Robert and Michael was as spacious as Brother Jaime's private quarters, but were meant for two rather than one. A table with four chairs sat in the middle of the room, a full skin of wine in the middle of it. The three sat around the table and each filled a goblet.

They glanced around and at each other as they sipped their wine. Robert broke the silence. "What do we do now?"

Michael shook his head sadly. "King Edward already has word out to find and bring before him the rogue Lord Alexander St. Clair. It will be all the incentive Brother Jaime needs to boot him out. And no Preceptor can ignore the commandments of a King."

Robert nodded in response.

Alexander looked up at Michael. "But you're a Master."

Now Michael nodded. "In Ireland. But we're in Scotland."

Alexander was almost panicked. "What if I offered myself as a Knight of the Order?"

Robert eyed him, suspicion alighting in his eyes. "Why would you want to do that? Just to escape the clutches of King Edward?"

Alex shook his head slowly, his eyes going introspective. "I've long admired the Order. And there is nothing left for me in Scotland. Perhaps, Brother Robert, I wish to dedicate my remaining life and vigor to deeds of more exalted usefulness." His eyes locked onto Robert's. "I seek the favor and hospitality of the Temple."

Their eyes locked on each other's, neither saw Michael's single sharp nod. "Then it's settled. Tomorrow, we start making our way to Dublin. There, you will be received into the bosom of the Temple."

Robert's head jerked to Michael. He looked shocked, then nodded, a grin creasing his features. "Master's prerogative?"

Now Michael grinned back. "That was my plan." He looked over at Alexander. "You will travel with me unimpeded even among the soldiers of King Edward. Until your formal Initiation, you are an Associate of the Order in Ireland and are under my personal protection as Master of the Temple in Ireland."

Robert nodded decisively. "Excellent, Worshipful Master."

Michael's grin was now impish as Alexander yawned. It was amazing how sure he felt now that the decision had been made. Michael told him, "Go to your rest, my boy. We've got a long journey starting tomorrow."

The three horses were saddled. It had been decided that Robert de Burghe, as Preceptor of Southern Scotland would accompany the Irish Master and his new/old charge to Dublin and there witness the Scotsman's Initiation. As the three men mounted their horses, a retinue of English soldiers, somehow alerted to the presence of Lord Alexander St. Clair, rode up and held up the small party.

"Lord Templar," he addressed the Preceptor, "this man is wanted by His Royal Britannic Majesty Edward of the House of Plantagenet, as a rebel against his royal authority. We request that you turn him over to us."

The Master of Ireland rode up next to the French Preceptor of Southern Scotland. "That will not be acceptable, Captain. This man is an Associate of the Temple in Ireland and will be Initiated at the first possible meeting of the Preceptory in Dublin. King Edward is invited to his public reception if he so wishes. Until he comes to seek Lord Alexander there himself, however, he is under my personal protection."

As the last words were spoken, a retinue of Templar knights came out to the side of the Irish Master and Scottish Preceptor. The English soldiers made no more attempts to capture Lord Alexander as the three rode away to the port.

The lines were cast off and the Templar galley made its way away from the docks outside Edinburgh. A crew of Templar sergeants rode below, to man oars in case the winds were not favorable.

Alexander looked up at the black ensign that flew above him, the skull set above crossed legbones, and felt truly safe for the first time since Fiona's death. He looked over at Lord Michael, Brother Michael, he corrected himself, who looked back at him with a wide smile. Alexander nodded back. He looked across the port and spotted the captain of English troops now in conversation with one of the men of the port, who obviously had little time, even for His Britannic Majesty's men.

Alexander raised his hand and waved to the English captain, who silently fumed at him from across the widening water.

Chapter 18

Increased activity on deck woke Alexander from a restful sleep. He pushed the blanket away and rose, making his way topside. The trip had taken most of two weeks. They were now under the power of the oarsmen and the Captain of the ship guided them into the dock.

A score of brown-clad sergeants was waiting for them, accompanied by six white-clad knights, all in full battle armor. Alex became aware of Michael and Robert standing beside him on the deck and was immediately grateful that he had taken their advice and put on the basic white robe that marked him as an Associate of the Temple.

Brother Michael, the Master of the Temple in Ireland, was also clad for combat, as was Brother Robert, the Preceptor for Southern Scotland. This was as close as Alexander had been to Templars in armor. The links of the chain mail under their tunics gleamed dully, even to the gauntlets at their wrists. Their tunics were snow-white with red crosses splayed on their chests. Silver thread was interwoven with the black belt around Robert's waist, which held a silver sheath and sword; while gold thread and metal decorated Michael. A white cloak was girded around each man's shoulders but bared the right shoulder while the left was covered by another blood-red cross that matched the ones on their chests. Black pants with leather chaps covered their legs while matching leather boots encased their feet. It was quite an effect.

The galley docked and a gangway was laid in place. Michael was the first off the ship and he was saluted by the lead knight among the Templars. Another salute was offered to Robert. When Michael reached back, Alexander was caught a little unawares as he was focusing on his new surroundings. The Master pulled him up to face the senior Templar.

He was bald with a thick beard and only one eye. The other was uncovered, the lid sunken into the socket. "Lord Alexander, this is Brother Jakob von Worms, the Commander of the Dublin Preceptory. He will be your host for the time. You will be permitted to rest for the rest of the night and tomorrow. At dawn on Thursday, you will be awakened and guided to prayers. After the noon meal that day, you will be publicly received by me into the Temple. That evening, well, you will see. But, for now, go with Brother Jakob." Michael turned to the thick German. "Brother Jakob, take good care of my old friend Alexander." With that, Michael and Robert turned and strode away, mounting nearby horses and riding off.

Alexander looked confused. "Where are they going?"

Jakob chuckled. "Temple business, I'm sure, Alexander. Now, come with me, please."

With that, Jakob led off toward the Dublin Preceptory, accompanied by the rest of the retinue. Alexander shrugged and followed.

Brother Jakob came into the Preceptory chapel, where Alexander prayed in the silence of the beautiful room. He was clad only in a long white robe and slippers. He kneeled before an open Bible, whose Latin he could easily translate, thanks to the lessons learned in Kincora so many years before. He looked up to see the Templar, clad in his ceremonial robes, and rose to follow him.

He had already taken the monk's vows of poverty, chastity, and obedience in the chapel. These had been administered in the presence of Jakob, Michael, and Robert by a Templar chaplain, who wore a green tunic with the Order's red cross patee and white gloves. Afterwards, he had exchanged the ritual embrace of peace with each of the Templars.

Now, he was led to the dining hall/meeting room of the Preceptory. The room was huge and full of brown-clad Templar sergeants, white-clad Templar knights, and green-clad Templar chaplains, who were segregated by their rank and all of whom were separated from the public. Alexander looked around and spotted several local nobles and clergy, including, he recognized, the Bishop of Dublin, who had been a part of Alex's life when he'd been at Kincora. The Scottish noble quickly realized that all eyes were on him.

Brother Michael sat in a large chair on a dais at the eastern end of the room. He spoke with authority that echoed his booming voice through the large room. "Brother Jakob, whom have you there in charge?"

The German's voice was just as authoritative. "Worshipful Master, I bring before you and this assembly Sir Alexander St. Clair, formerly of Roslin in the kingdom of Scotland. He seeks the hospitality of the House and to become a Poor Fellow-Soldier of Christ and the Temple of Solomon."

Michael nodded. "Sir Alexander, is this request made of your own free will and accord?"

As he had been instructed, Alexander answered. "It is."

"Brother Jakob, who stands forth to vouch for his character?"

The French-accented voice of Brother Robert de Burghe sounded from a chair near Michael's. "I will vouch for him, Worshipful Master."

Michael smiled and nodded but quickly covered his face with a severe look. "Sir Alexander, you no doubt have long considered your desire to join with our Order. But it is my duty at this time to inform you that the life you ask for is not one of ease. It is one of tireless and endless service, a preparation for the service which we will no doubt render to our Father in Heaven and His Son. You see merely the outer existence of the Order, our shining armor, grand steeds, and immaculate buildings. But, when you join with us, you must follow the orders of your superiors in the Order. When you wish to lay down and sleep, you may be ordered to stand watch. When you wish to fast, you may be ordered to eat. And when you wish to stay in one place, you may be ordered to the farthest reaches of Christendom. With this admonition, do you still wish to join with us in our service?"

"Worshipful Master, I will suffer all that is pleasing to Christ and our Heavenly Father." This, too, had been part of Jakob's instructions.

Michael stood and advanced to stand before Alexander. "With this hand, you are formally welcomed into this Preceptory as a Poor Fellow-Soldier of Christ and the Temple of Solomon." The two men's hands touched in a brace, followed by a tight embrace between the warriors. The assembled crowd rose to its feet and applauded the creation of one more Templar.

The sun had gone down and Alexander had been ordered alone to this room for the night. He had thought that he would be put in the general barracks with the other knights, but found himself unable to complain. He kneeled to pray, clad only in a plain white robe, as that was still all he had. The knock on the door surprised him.

He rose and opened the door, to find Brother Jakob again at the threshold. Two other Templar knights brushed into the room past him and held him fast. He struggled briefly against their grip but Jakob's shining blade stopped him. "Be calm, Brother Alexander. There is more to this than meets the eye." The Commander wrapped a blindfold around his head, taking him into darkness.

He was led through the Preceptory to a door. He had no clue where the door was but felt his hand pulled from his side. "You now stand outside the Asylum of the Temple. Make a fist," a whispered voice told him. He did so and his fist was struck against a door three times. As he struck the door each time, the whispered, unfamiliar voice stated a sentence. "Ask and it shall be given you. Seek and ye shall find. Knock and it shall be opened unto you. Matthew Chapter 7, Verse 7."

Alexander could hear the door open. "Who comes here?" This was a Germanic voice, the Preceptor of Leinster, the province that held Dublin.

His guide answered for him. "Alexander macEdward St. Clair, a blind stranger who desires to come from the dark to the light by receiving a part of the rights of this Asylum of Poor Fellow-Soldiers of Christ and the Temple of Solomon."

The door closed and there were muted voices from within. Without warning, the door again opened. "It is the command of the Worshipful Master that the stranger enter."

Alexander was led into the room, where he was stopped short. The neck of his robe was pulled down and a sharp point was pressed to the left side of his chest. "Sir Alexander, you are here received upon the point of the dagger in your naked left breast, which is to teach you to suffer all that is pleasing to Christ and as a reminder of the pain your heart should feel should you ever attempt to reveal the secrets of the Order or your brethren." The dagger was removed and Alex could feel a trickle of blood down his chest.

Now he was led out by his guide. He was told to kneel and the voice of Brother Michael intoned a brief prayer that was directed to the Almighty Father. The prayer was in Latin.

He was led in a big circle, it seemed, then made to face the voice of Brother Michael. He was instructed then to kneel on his left knee. His left hand was guided out, palm up, and a book was pressed onto it. His right hand was guided out and placed palm down on top of that same book.

Brother Michael spoke, telling him to repeat the oath as he spoke it. "I, Michael O'Brian, of my own free will, in the presence of the Almighty Grand Master of Heaven and these my Brethren, do hereby solemnly promise and swear that I will forever keep the secrets of the Order of the Temple and my Brethren.

"I promise that I will never write on anything that can show a mark any of the orders received from my superior but will learn their lessons that they may be passed on to my less-informed Brethren.

"I swear this, my oath, as an Entrant of the Order of the Temple. And I invite my Brethren to punish me suitably should I violate this oath by slitting my throat open and tearing out my tongue, before burying my body in unconsecrated ground by the sea where the tide will cover me twice a day. So help me, Father."

Michael ordered Alexander to kiss the Bible in his hands to seal his oath. He then told him to arise, which he did. Michael asked, "My Brother, what do you now desire?"

The guide's voice in his ear instructed him to answer, "Light."

Michael issued his orders. "Brother Seneschal and Brother Marshal, assist me."

Suddenly, the blindfold was pulled from his eyes. Michael stood in the middle of the three with Robert on his right and Jakob on his left. All three held their hands in the same position Alex's hands had been while he took the oath, but without the Bible between them. As one, they dropped their left hands to their sides then raised their right to slice across their throats.

Robert and Jakob returned to seats, Robert in a seat behind the Altar where Alexander stood and Jakob to Alexander's right. Michael remained standing where he was and presently, began to speak. "You now behold me, my Brother, approaching you from the East and I will explain to you the signs of an Entrant of the Temple. This is the guard, the position in which your hands were placed when you took your oath." The first position of the hands was again displayed. "And this is the sign, and reminds you that you invited your Brethren to slit your throat open and so on." He drew his right hand again across his throat. "These signs will allow you to prove yourself a true Entrant of the Temple to any who may question it." He then took a white object off of the podium behind him. "I now present you with your lambskin. This you will wear always as a Knight of the Temple. It is an emblem of innocence and the badge of a Templar. It is the most sacred honor that can be given you by any person, even the Pope, except by a Brother. Wear it with pleasure to yourself and honor to the Order." The lambskin was girded around his waist. With that, Michael came around the Altar and embraced him again. "Now you are truly my Brother, Alexander."

Chapter 19

Brother Alexander had settled into a normal routine. He shared a large sleeping room with three other Templar knights. Each maintained his bunk and area in a severe manner. Every morning, they were given their instructions for the day. They generally spent half of the day patrolling somewhere in Dublin where they acted as a reserve to the local bailiff. The other half of the day was dedicated to training and prayer. After their evening meal, which was held in strict silence, the only sound being the voice of one of the chaplains reading from the Holy Scriptures. After supper, each knight was to see to his mount and equipment, making sure that his weapons were clean and rust-free, ready at a moment's notice to be sent elsewhere for combat duty or pressed into service in Ireland. Meanwhile, he kept his hair cut close and allowed his beard to grow thick on his chin.

Within weeks of his arrival, word arrived that the Grand Master, Jacques de Molay, in Cyprus had appointed a new Master in England. Brother Robert de Burghe was awarded the golden thread of his new office and set sail for London, where he would begin his service. The morning after he sailed, Alexander was awakened early to ride with the Irish Master.

The two old friends rode companionably in silence for a time, enjoying each other's friendship and company. Michael finally chuckled.

"Several of the other Entrants, of which we have more than our share here in peaceful Ireland, wish to know when I will take you to Kincora to serve at my right hand. I hate to tell you that this is not yet possible."

Alexander nodded by way of response. "I will serve the Order in any way in which I can, Worshipful Master."

Michael was more than pleased at Alexander's proper response. "Robert wanted to take you to London. He thought it would be a good way to tweak King Edward's nose." He paused for a chuckle. "He knows as well as I do, however, that you must raise yourself in rank before any higher assignment may come your way."

Alexander looked out of the corner of his eye at his mentor. Michael continued. "The Order values combat experience above all else. Therefore, I am sending you to the service of Brother Thibauld de Paris, the Master of the Temple in Castile. As you know, Castile continues to fight the Moors. There you will see real combat, you will become a Fellow of the Order, rather than just an Entrant. You will be placed in a position of leadership if you are successful."

"What if I'm not successful?"

Michael grinned widely. "Then, old friend, you will be dead."

Alexander stopped his horse in surprise. That hadn't really occurred to him.

When the galley pulled alongside the dock at Bilbao, most of Alexander's baggage was lifted by the two sergeants who had been assigned to him by Brother Michael. They, too, were being transferred to the Castilian command, to serve as his assistants. One was a grizzled old veteran named Brian O'Carroll, an Irishman, while the other was a fresh recruit named Eric Smythe, an Englishman.

It had been interesting watching them and seeing how Brian had reacted not only to their English compatriot, but also how he'd reacted to his newly-assigned knight. Alexander knew that, in addition to being a sergeant, Brian was also a Fellow of the Order. Since he'd heard Michael's allusion to that, he had wondered at its meaning, but no definite definition was forthcoming. Still, Brian was deferential to Alexander, but continued to associate more with the combat veterans on board the galley. He basically ignored Eric unless giving him a direct order or correcting something he'd done wrong. Alexander silently cursed. He was still too new to the Temple to really understand what was going on. Also silently, he girded himself to meet a new companion, who would be waiting on the docks.

The gangplank was dropped into place and Alexander, as the only knight aboard the galley, led the way across. Brothers Brian and Eric followed him. Two sergeants, their swarthy looks and dark hair suggesting a mixed heritage, met them. They stood next to a two-horse wagon and, when they spotted the arrivals from Dublin, they snapped to attention. One of them snapped a salute to Alexander.

"Brother Knight," he began, "I am Brother Eduardo and this is Brother Gregorio. We serve Brother Knight Joseph, who has stepped away to tend to personal business."

Alexander returned the salute. "I am Brother Alexander. These sergeants are Brother Brian and Brother Eric." He indicated each of them as they bowed, as their burdens allowed, to the other sergeants.

Eduardo stepped forward and gestured to the wagon. "You may place your luggage on the wagon." Alexander supervised the loading as they waited for the arrival of the Spanish knight. He was surprised when a Templar approached who appeared to be an Arab. He wore an obvious armor under his tunic that looked to be thinner than the mail that was part of Alex's luggage, but that Alex had been told not to wear until directed to do so by a compatriot in Castile. He also wore a conical helmet and wore a thin, curved sword on his left hip, which was far different from the helms and swords that Alex was more familiar with. The Arabic Templar extended his hand and gave Alex the proper token, the grip given by which a Brother could recognize another in the dark or the light. "Good day, my Brother. I am Joseph, the Turcopolier of Castile, and have been sent by the Worshipful Brother Thibauld to welcome you to Castile and bring you to his Preceptory in Madrid."

Alexander remained slightly confused, but acquiesced to the obvious command of Brother Joseph, who had Gregorio bring two traveling horses. He explained, as Alex mounted the gelding he had been brought, that it would take them a few days to reach Madrid, but they would have safe-houses in the various Preceptories and among other religious houses they would reach along the way. Brian used his higher standing to secure himself a seat on the bench next to Eduardo, forcing Gregorio and Eric to ride in the back of the wagon.

The two knights rode ahead as the wagon followed. Alex could bear his curiosity no longer and began to speak to his compatriot. "Brother Joseph, please excuse my ignorance as I am new to the Order, but what is a Turcopolier?"

Joseph grinned under his thick beard. "How many Preceptories have you served in?"

"Only in Dublin, in Ireland. But I lived around the Preceptories in Edinburgh and Roslin in Scotland."

"No reason you should know, my Brother. So far as I am aware, there are only *turcopoles* in the Iberian nations any more. They used to have them in Outremer, but, of course, no longer. A *turcopole* is a light infantry warrior. We wear lighter armor and different helmets and are a corps made up mainly of sergeants. One knight in each Preceptory with a *turcopole* corps is denoted the Turcopolier and is the commanding officer of the *turcopole* corps."

Alex nodded, recognizing that they would seem to be a regional troop, similar to his own "heavy infantry" of axe-bearers in Scotland. "Do you have special training to serve as a Turcopolier, my Brother?"

Joseph's grin held easily. "I have been a *turcopole* my entire Templar career. I started out as a sergeant, but won my knighthood through honor on the field of combat, as I had to take command of my corps in battle against the Moors six years ago. Since I had to be a knight to become permanent Turcopolier, I was granted a knighthood by the King of Castile at the desire of the Master at the time. When Worshipful Brother Thibauld became Master of Castile two years ago, he appointed me to remain in my post."

Alex nodded, impressed by Joseph's story. "Are you Spanish, Joseph?"

Joseph laughed easily, his strange accent gaining more currency. "No, Alexander. I am a Syrian."

This caused Alex to straighten in his saddle. "Syrian?"

Joseph nodded. "Yes. I was born in Damascus to Muslim parents and named Yousif, after Jesus' adoptive father. They emigrated from Syria to Constantinople when I was a boy. They were killed in a raid by, ironically enough, Syrian troops. I was adopted by a young princess who had been widowed without children. I was doted on by my grandfather and mother and they made sure that I was apprenticed to a rich, powerful merchant. But I was a wild boy who wanted adventure and admired the powerful Templars, even the sergeants, who came through Constantinople and other places where my master took me. So, when I reached my majority, rather than taking the money and career that were waiting for me, I ran off to the nearest Preceptory and swore allegiance to the Temple, asking for the hospitality of the House. It was granted and I was immediately sent to Madrid, where I was enlisted as a *turcopole*, and, eventually, I gained the status that I told you of."

He turned to Alex. "What about you?"

Alex had not really thought to tell his story but it rolled out of him. By the time he was done, the sun sat heavily on the horizon. Luckily, by planning actually, they had reached a small monastery and Joseph motioned for him to wait. Joseph dismounted and Gregorio took his mount's reins as he strolled up to the door, knocking confidently on the gate. The monk guarding the gate embraced Joseph and, in minutes, the gates were opened and the Templar contingent was welcomed in.

The sergeants were commanded to see to the horses and the two knights were directed to a room where they were served by the brothers of the monastery and ate in silence. When they were finished dining, they were joined by the sergeants and Joseph led them all in evening prayers.

The sergeants departed for their quarters while the two knights removed their robes, down to the lambskins, which they did not remove, and laid down, a lamp still burning, to go to sleep.

As dreamland approached, a question occurred to Alex, one he'd been fairly dying to ask. "Brother Joseph, what is a Fellow of the Order?"

Joseph sighed. Apparently, he had guessed that Alex had no reason to know this information. "You do not need to know, Brother Entrant. Now go to sleep."

Alexander started to be offended by the reply, but also knew of the Templar compunction for following orders. He stifled his own sigh and responded. "Yes, Brother Joseph." Within minutes, the Arabic Templar was snoring softly. Somewhat to his surprise, at least in his dreams, shortly thereafter, Alexander was as well.

Chapter 20

Within several days, the pair of knights led the wagon into the gates of the Madrid Preceptory. They were greeted as Brothers should be and quickly Alexander's gear was taken to the Preceptory's armory, where some goods were replaced and everything was recorded into the inventory by the Brother Draper, a severe Frenchmen named Etienne de Marseilles.

Having explored his quarters, which he shared with three other knights, one of whom was Joseph, he was led into the great hall, where the Master of Castile awaited him.

Brother Thibauld de Paris was tall and spare. His head was shorn so closely as to be reflective of the light and his beard was neatly trimmed and dark. He wore the gold threading and extras that marked his consequence. Also present in the room was Prince Enrique, one of the lesser sons of the King of Castile, who was known to be highly supportive of the Templars and their efforts to expel the Moors from the territory of Iberia.

Alexander came forward and bowed low. Brother Joseph accompanied him and spoke for him. "Worshipful Master, I take pleasure in presenting to you Brother Alexander St. Clair, an Entrant of the Order late of the Preceptory of Dublin in Ireland, now assigned to your command here in Madrid in Castile."

Thibauld regarded Alexander coolly. "Brother Alexander, a couple of weeks ago, I received a letter from Worshipful Brother Michael in Ireland. I was quite impressed by your pedigree and experience, even if some of it was against such a proponent of our Order as His Britannic Majesty Edward." He chuckled as the sarcasm dripped from his tongue. Edward was well-known for his ambivalence toward the Order. He basically seemed to be of the opinion that he could manage the Temple far better than the Templars, a belief that King Philip IV in France also seemed to have. "So, tell me, Brother Alexander, do you seek to do battle as soon as practicable?"

Alexander barely considered for a moment and did everything possible to hide his eagerness. "I will serve whenever and wherever I am sent, Worshipful Master."

Thibauld's laugh was as spare as his appearance, but still conveyed his pleasure. "They did teach you manners in Dublin, but I expected that from so fine a Master as Michael." His eyes flicked past Alexander to Joseph. "Brother Turcopolier, your men await you in the field. A band of roving Moorish bandits waits to face our troops on the morrow. Take our Brother Alexander and introduce him to the Brother Marshal, who will no doubt find a way to use him well." His eyes returned to Alexander. "Good luck, my dear Brother Alexander. Tomorrow, you will participate in what our Muslim foes describe as *jihad*, holy war. If you survive, you may yet go far in service to the Temple. If you do not, your soul will find Heaven but your bones will never return to your native Scotland."

Alexander bowed again at his dismissal, wondering exactly what he might have gotten himself into.

Alexander dismounted in the morning and was led by the sergeant, Brother Gregorio, to the tent of Brother Adolph von Trieste, the Marshal of Castile. Upon making an introduction to Brother Adolph's senior servant, the Spanish *turcopole* rode off to join his fellows. Alexander was accompanied by Brother Eric Smythe, who carried his lance while he wore the armor of the heavy cavalryman.

Upon entering the tent, they found Brother Adolph looking over a map on a table. It was a familiar scene for the Scottish knight as he was used to planning operations such as this. Adolph was younger than Alexander and was obviously perplexed by how to best disperse his forces. Alexander found himself instinctively wanting to help the Lotharingian Templar he had yet to formally meet.

Adolph's senior sergeant was a Spaniard named Brother Rodrigo de Santa Clara. Rodrigo was also the field commander of the infantry and was experienced both in command and in planning operations. He was also perplexed at how his commander could have trouble with the planning of what should be a simple defense against a large band of Moorish bandits. He now led the new arrivals to the table.

"Brother Adolph," bowed Rodrigo. "This is Brother Knight Alexander St. Clair and Brother Sergeant Eric Smythe. They are newly arrived and assigned to your command by Worshipful Brother Thibauld."

Adolph moved around the table and took each new Brother by the hand. "Welcome to Castile. Brother Eric, you will be assigned to Brother Rodrigo's infantry. Brother Alexander, the cavalry is currently assigned to the right of our formation." He turned away in dismissal, returning his attention to the map.

Brother Alexander couldn't help himself. "Brother Adolph, do you require assistance?" His hand motioned to the table.

A flare of distrust in his eyes, Adolph's voice was a little hot. "Do you believe I do not know about strategy, Brother Alexander?"

Alexander had learned enough diplomacy among the Scottish barons to know how to respond. "By no means would I ever suggest such a thing, my Brother. I am an experienced field commander and merely wish to offer my assistance to what is no doubt a fine plan."

Adolph was a bit taken aback by the quick response but found himself admiring the Scot's answer and hoping he was as good as he presented himself to be.

He turned to Rodrigo. "Brother Rodrigo, escort Brother Eric to his position. Your orders will be coming directly." He turned back to the newly-arrived knight. "Brother Alexander, please stay and speak with me. My plan is nearly complete but would doubtless be improved by another experienced hand."

The battle ended in victory, Alexander found that the Templars celebrated much like other soldiers, just without the women. He also found that he didn't mind the lack of female companionship. He did find his heart aching a bit for Fiona, but it was now a distant ache, much like the scars he had collected through a life of warfare. They ached dully, but the sharpness of a fresh wound was long gone.

Still, there was ale and mead and fresh beef from a slaughtered cow. They conspicuously roasted and ate pork in the presence of Moorish prisoners, whose Islamic faith forbade them the meat of the pig. Alexander took his turn at taunting them, chained as they were. He was amazed that he had been so frightened of them before the battle, when he had first seen them, alien as they were to what he was used to, but now he showed that fear conquered by laughing at them, waving the chops and wine in their bearded faces.

He soberly realized that he could never question their courage or their ability. They had proven themselves warriors of fine mettle and he distantly worried about the next time he would face such men, or finer men, who were real soldiers, not the bandits he knew these men to be.

These questions were banished by the joy and laughter of Brother Adolph. As Alexander had earlier suspected, this was his first battle as commander of these forces, his first as Marshal. That it had been a great success was a measure of his ability and willingness to listen to those who had the experience, if not the rank. Adolph pounded Alexander on the back, thanking him more than once for his own role in the day's proceedings.

The looks he got from the other knights, distrustful at first as they would be in any military company, the newcomer among the veterans, were now friendly. Nods of respect and camaraderie were plentiful, as word got around that the new arrival had assisted in planning. Obviously, he was a figure to respect and his use of the *turcopoles* had the veteran knights granting the sergeants a new esteem.

Alexander noticed as sergeants and knights started to come to attention. He quickly saw the newly-arrived Master of Castile. He, too, leaped to his feet, coming to strict attention to salute Brother Thibauld. Adolph, on his left, did the same.

The Frenchman regarded the Marshal and the Scotsman with an approving look. "Brother Adolph, a great victory has proven your skill. I salute your skill."

Adolph bowed deeply at the compliment. "I thank you, Worshipful Master. But our victory may not have come without the advice of Brother Alexander." Adolph nodded toward the Scotsman and the Master turned his attention there.

"Brother Alexander, all that Worshipful Brother Michael told us to expect seems to be more than true. He spoke highly of your personal courage and of your martial ability. I am proud to write back to him on the morn of your proving his points."

Alexander bowed at Thibauld's words. "I thank you, also, Worshipful Master."

Thibauld smiled broadly. "Now, if someone will get me a tankard, we will celebrate further."

The Master's wish was carried out.

They came for him in the night. He had not celebrated as hard as many of them, just enough to feel good. When they woke him from a dead sleep, however, he didn't feel very good.

They were clad in the white robes of Templars. He was wearing his lambskin, which was all that was left of his clothing after he had stripped himself for bed. They half-drug, half-carried him to a tent at the center of the encampment. A Templar with a drawn sword guarded the tent flap, which was tightly closed.

"Clap three times," came the harsh order. Again, he recognized the voice of one he knew, this time Brother Joseph. Alexander shook his head to clear it. The Syrian Templar cuffed him in the back of the head. "Do it!"

Alexander clapped his hands three times. The tent flap opened and he was led inside. Thibauld sat in a throne at the head of the tent. Others sat with him. Alexander was aware of Brother Knights around the room, all of them men he had fought with this day except for the Master of Castile and the man who sat on the back wall of the tent. He had only one eye but had the swarthy darkness of one of mixed Spanish and Arabian blood. Alexander would later find that this was Brother Pedro San Francisco, the Seneschal or second-in-command of the Order in Castile. He was the product of a marriage between a Christian Spanish noble and the daughter of an Arabian trader who had converted to the Faith. Brother Adolph sat midway between the ends of the tent to the left of Thibauld and the right of Pedro.

Joseph whispered in Alexander's ear. "Relax and follow me." His strong hand gripped Alexander's wrist and he led him around the room twice. They stopped before Brother Adolph, who asked, "Who comes here?"

Joseph's voice was strong. "Brother Alexander St. Clair, an Entrant of the Order, who has proved himself in battle and now desires to be passed to the rank of Fellow."

"Brother Alexander, is this of your own will and accord?"

Joseph's hand prodded the Scot. "It is," he said.

"Brother Conductor, is the Brother duly and truly prepared?"

Joseph's voice again. "He is."

"Is he worthy and qualified?"

"He is."

"By what right does he expect to gain passage?"

"Be the pass."

"Does he have the pass?"

"He does not, but I have it for him."

"Prove it."

Joseph stepped forward and whispered something in his ear. Adolph nodded. "He may pass."

Alexander was led to Pedro, then to Thibauld, where the ceremony was repeated. Then he was led to the Altar in the center of the room, where rested a Bible. Alexander was made to kneel on his right knee, to raise his left arm and place his right hand on the Bible. Brother Thibauld administered the oath, which Alexander repeated.

"I, Thibauld of Paris, of my own free will, in the presence of the Almighty Grand Master of Heaven and these my Brethren, do hereby solemnly promise and swear that I will forever keep the secrets of the Order of the Temple and my Brethren.

"I promise that I will follow the Rule of the Order to death.

"I promise that I will answer the summons of my superiors of the Order, if at all possible to do so.

"I promise that I will always aid a Brother of the Temple.

"And I promise that I will never cheat or wrong a Brother of the Temple out of the value of anything, nor permit it to be done if I may prevent it.

"I swear this, my oath, as a Fellow of the Order of the Temple. And I invite my Brethren to punish me suitably should I violate this oath by tearing open my left breast and casting my heart and vitals to serve as a prey to the vultures of the air and the beasts of the field. So help me, Father."

Again, Alexander was ordered to kiss the Bible before him. Again he arose from his kneeling position. Again, he was asked the questions, "My Brother, what do you now desire?"

This time, the answer was not whispered into his ear, but he remembered how to respond. "Light."

Thibauld answered. "Brother Seneschal and Brother Marshal, assist me."

The blindfold was removed from his eyes and he beheld Thibauld, Pedro, and Adolph before him. Their right hands were extended forward, resting on imaginary Bibles, while their lefts were extended out, raised above shoulder level. Their right hands moved, as though tearing across the left side of their chests. Pedro and Adolph returned to their seats, while Thibauld remained. The words he spoke were again familiar. . "You now behold me, my Brother, approaching you from the East and I will explain to you the signs of a Fellow of the Temple. This is the guard, the position in which your hands were placed when you took your oath." The first position of the hands was again displayed. "And this is the sign, and reminds you that you invited your Brethren to tear open your left breast and so forth." He drew his right hand again across his chest. "These signs will allow you to prove yourself a true Fellow of the Temple to any who may question it."

Thibauld came forward and exchanged a ritual embrace with Alexander. "Welcome to a new world, my Brother."

Chapter 21

Alexander rose from his knees before Thibauld. Night reigned outside the Templar Preceptory in Madrid, home of the Master of the Temple in Castile. There were only eight knights in the Asylum. One, Brother Joseph, stood to Alexander's left. Thibauld, Pedro, and Adolph stood in the East of the Asylum. Brothers Arturo di Napoli, Preceptor of Aragon; William Saulsbury, Preceptor of Navarre; Connor O'Sitric, Preceptor of Leon; and Phillipe de Montreaux, Commander of Madrid; also stood as witnesses to this ultimate ranking ceremony within the Order of the Temple.

He had actually been warned of this one beforehand, that he was to be raised as a Master of the Order. Henceforth, his orders could not be questioned under any circumstances by any stationed below him. This was a rank that was not even guessed at by those who had been Initiated as Entrants and Passed as Fellows. He had been told of it by Brother Adolph, who had requested that he be named Deputy Marshal of the Temple in Castile.

The Brethren gathered around him now. A black cloth covered his eyes as the other Templars held his arms and legs fast. He was shoved along a path, confronted by a now-unseen assailant.

"Tell me the Rule of the Temple." The voice was unrecognizable and hissed darkly at him.

"I will not." Brother Joseph still stood beside him.

A cold blade, the flat of it, pressed against his throat then was gone. Again he was shoved along and stopped.

A second voice assaulted him. "Tell me the Rule of the Temple."

Again, Joseph. "I will not."

The second voice hissed again. "Tell me your orders as a Templar."

"I can not."

Something hard pressed against his chest, the back of an axe. Then it disappeared. Alexander was again pressed along the path. A long time he was forced before being stopped a third time. "Tell me the Rule of the Temple."

Joseph's voice a third time. "I will not."

"Tell me your orders as a Templar."

"I can not."

"Tell me the secrets of the Order."

"I will never reveal them and lose my integrity."

"Then, die."

Stars exploded in Alexander's vision as a heavy bag struck him in the forehead. His balance left him and he fell backwards. His brethren caught him, however, and lowered him gently to the ground.

Thibauld's voice rang strong and true in Alexander's darkened world. "This is your duty, my Brother. You may never reveal what you know of the Temple. Remain silent that our needs and the will of your Master will be forever hidden from those who would seek to destroy our Order, our Holy Church, even our faith. And, should you follow these commands now revealed to you, you may again be raised to life by the Grand Master of Heaven, our beloved Savior, the Lion of the Tribe of Judah." With these words, Thibauld took him in a bracing grip and pulled him to his feet, assisted by the other Templars. As he gained his feet, his eyes were uncovered. He beheld his Brother Templars and Thibauld turned him to look back at the place he had just laid.

A black cloth was there, a white skull and crossbones stitched onto it.

"For if you violate your vows, the darkness of the grave may very well be your eternity." This was said in the most solemn voice that Alexander had heard from Thibauld in his five years of service with the Temple. Now, the Master's face broke into a smile. "But you wouldn't do that, to us or yourself. Congratulations, Alexander." With that, the two men embraced warmly. More embraces followed as the others, all men who respected and had fought alongside the Scot, gave him their greetings. Now, he was entitled to know all that the Temple knew, if it pleased his superiors. Now, he truly knew what it was to be a Templar.

Thibauld sat in his high throne as Master in Castile. Sergeants, chaplains, and knights gathered around the assembled as Adolph led Alexander into the assembly room. Both Templars bowed deeply before straightening.

Adolph's already-blond beard had been bleached almost white by the sun of Spain. He stood erect, dark eyes twinkling, his strong right hand flexing. His left had fallen victim to a Moorish axe three months before. In most men, this would have occasioned his relief from combat duties, and Alexander would most likely have been elevated to his post then. But Adolph had become a strong field commander and showed little in the way of impairment with such a grisly injury. So, Thibauld had allowed him to remain in his post, but requested that he appoint a deputy. That choice was obvious to all who knew of the Templars' successes in Castile and elsewhere on the Iberian Peninsula. Alexander St. Clair was rapidly becoming a legend, even to the point of having been noticed favorably by such luminaries in the Order as Hugh de Pairaud, the Visitor in Paris and Treasurer of the Order, and even Jacques de Molay himself. It was whispered that Alexander might be called away and given the office of Grand Marshal of the Order, once he'd proved himself as a national Marshal.

Brother Thibauld began to speak. "Brother Marshal, you have requested to speak to this assembly. What have you to bring before us?"

Adolph's voice was clear and powerful. "Worshipful Master, I present Brother Alexander St. Clair, who I wish to name as my Deputy Marshal for Castile."

All eyes fell on the transplanted Scot. His beard had grown thick on his face, dark red with just the first streaks of white. Likewise, the stubble on his head, cut close in the manner of the Order, showed some streaks of new color. But it was the pale blue eyes that told the story. They had become harder to read, more intelligent, and even stronger in the five years he had spent fighting Moors, Arabs, and Saracens in Castile and even leading raids into north Africa. It was said that the Caliph of Cordoba had put a high price on his head and that said price went up further on a monthly basis, as Brother Alexander led more and more raids on Moorish lands. His frame, over six feet, stood erect before the Master of Castile. Obvious muscle stretched and bunched under his tunic and cloak. A silver-hilted sword hung on a silver-threaded belt around his trim waist, a waist that broadened to powerful shoulders that displayed pronounced strength. Thibauld nodded his approval.

"Very well, my Brother." He turned to the Secretary, a chaplain. "Let it be written and published that Brother Alexander St. Clair will serve as Deputy Marshal to Brother Adolph von Trieste." The Secretary nodded absently, already writing the order that would go out to all Templar Preceptories in Castile and to the Masters of other nations, as well as to the Grand Officers, wherever dispersed.

Thibauld turned back to the pair. "You are dismissed."

Alexander sat high in his saddle, inspecting the Moorish vanguard through a spyglass. He lowered it and looked over to report to his superior, concerned at the Lotharingian's appearance.

The German, already fair of skin, was downright pale, his skin having a grayish tinge that Alexander really didn't like. He was aware that Adolph had already weathered several infections due to his injury, but he worried that more might be coming.

"Brother Adolph," he said gently.

Adolph's head turned slowly to examine the Scot. His voice was a little dreamy. "Yes, Brother Alexander?"

"The Moors' strength is their center. I urge a flanking attack with the *turcopoles* against their right and our heavy cavalry against their left. Between the two, and with our infantry advancing against their middle, we should roll them right up."

The German shook his head, trying to clear it. "That sounds like a fine plan, my Brother. Send out the orders. I will lead the heavy cavalry myself. You will command."

Concern not for the plan, but for Adolph's safety, surfaced in Alexander's pale blue eyes. His hand reached across to Adolph's shoulder. "Are you sure, Brother?"

Adolph shook his hand away, his eyes burning. "Of course I am sure, Deputy. It will be a fine victory." He turned his horse and rode away.

Joseph tracked the Lotharingian Templar with his eyes. "I believe our Marshal wishes to perish on the morrow."

Alexander nodded his head absently. "I believe you may be right, Brother Turcopolier."

The morning dawned crisp and hot on the Castilian plain. Alexander viewed the disposition of Templar troops, supplemented by soldiers from several of the surrounding noble lords. The Moors aligned against them were a strong force, the strongest in the time that Alexander had served here.

Joseph held his *turcopoles* under strong control. The mounted sergeants had become the pride of the Castilian Temple, followed closely by the heavy infantry that Alexander had brought from Scotland and Ireland. The axe-bearing sergeants could mow through any infantry they faced. And the Christian center included two full schiltrons of dismounted lance-bearers, whose long reach could decimate the mounted Moorish heavy cavalry. Alexander allowed himself a small smile. He had trained those men himself and had also pushed for the importation of the archers from Wales. Next, Alexander's eyes found Adolph, looking grayer than the day before on his horse. He had assigned Brother Kenneth Taggart, his cousin, though the younger knight did not know it, to second Brother Adolph. Kenneth was an intelligent and well-trained cavalryman, who was aware of Adolph's fatalism. It is hard to hide such things from good soldiers. And all of the men in the Templar force were good soldiers.

They had also copied Alexander's confidence. His strength in planning and ordering execution of combat forces was second to none in Castile, at least so it was widely believed. Most of the senior knights knew that he had long been Adolph's chief aide when it came to planning attacks and had been behind much of the innovation seen in recent Templar ranks.

Now, he stared across the field at the Moorish warriors, beating their chest and letting out high, ululating screams of war. He turned to his aide, Sergeant Eric Smythe. "Archers," he ordered softly.

Eric turned his horse in place and shouted. "Archers!"

A flag-bearer waved the proper flag and the Welsh bowmen stepped forward. As they raised their bows and let fly with the first volley, the battle commenced.

Alexander rested outside his tent, awaiting the attention of a surgeon to repair the long cut at his left collarbone. The Moor who had dealt it had long been dispatched to the infernal regions. That must have been a shock, thought the Deputy Marshal of Castile, expecting dewy-eyed virgins, but being greeted by Lucifer himself.

He grinned darkly at the memory of the feel of the Moor's flesh parting under his blade. He had actually thrilled to the sight of the life leaving the other man's eyes. The medical man came forward and poured pure alcohol over the wound on his neck. It stung but Alexander forced himself not to react. A needle and thin thread went to work on the short slash and the surgeon, a Sergeant of the Temple, quickly closed the wound. Another treatment of alcohol, this time the drinking kind to help dull the pain, and he was up to see to other wounded men.

He stepped into the tent and looked upon Adolph von Trieste. The Marshal was now well into his death throes. He had veritably thrown himself at the Moorish forces and been rewarded by being sliced to shreds by their blades. One of his legs was already gone and his torso was marked by a score or more of cuts. It was a tribute to his toughness that he still breathed, but all present knew that he was not long for this world.

Alexander's head turned as Thibauld de Paris entered the tent. He had sent for the Master in Castile as the battle ended, but not expected his arrival until morning. Alexander bowed deeply. "Worshipful Master," he intoned.

Thibauld nodded tiredly. "What's the story, Brother Alexander?"

"He is well and truly dying, Worshipful. I believe it was his wish."

Another nod. "So Brother Joseph told me." He walked over to the table that held Adolph and set his hand on his friend's shoulder. He leaned down and whispered something into the younger man's ear. Then he straightened and turned to Alexander. "I know this is not how you could have wanted this, but I hereby appoint you Marshal of the Temple in Castile." He bowed his head. "And may you lead and fight bravely against all enemies of Christ and Holy Mother Church. Amen."

Alexander muttered, "So mote it be."

Chapter 22

Templar Knight Sir Eric Smythe rode at the head of the line into the rainy Paris night. For four years, he had supported and aided the Marshal of the Temple in Castile, rarely resting during the campaigning season, rarely resting even between them as he trained himself and other men. Now it was June 1307 and the Most Worshipful Brother Jacques de Molay had appointed his commander to appear at the Paris Commandery, there to meet with Brother Geoffrey de Charney, Preceptor of Normandy, who had recently arrived from Cyprus.

Alexander St. Clair's tenure as Marshal had been an unqualified success. Templar arms had known no greater successes than they had met under his command. And Eric Smythe had become an unqualified success as a field commander as well, leading infantry against Moors, then gaining training as a *turcopole*. When Brother Joseph was made Seneschal at Pedro's reassignment in 1305 as Master in Bavaria, they had needed a new Turcopolier. Both Joseph and Alexander recommended him to Brother Thibauld. He had been bathed and prayed over, as befit his status as a Templar, then knighted by the sword of Brother Alexander himself. He would ride anywhere to support his patron, and support him to any end.

So, when Thibauld had relayed Alexander's orders to Paris, Eric had requested to go as well. He did not know what he might be assigned to do, and really did not care He merely wished to continue as he had in his mentor's service for the last nine years.

Alexander, meanwhile, was also introspective as he rode through the rain. His beard had gained more white with four more years and more responsibility. But he was still powerfully-built with broad shoulders and a barrel chest. He still had drawn more glances from women at court in Madrid than most other Templars, even though he had never taken advantage of their silent invitations. He knew that made him somewhat rare, even among the Brethren of the Temple. Despite their excellent reputations, they were still human, and still men. He sighed softly into his beard.

His eyes brightened as they gained sight of the Paris Preceptory. Eric called up a sergeant. "Brother Pietro, go forward and inform the guard at the Preceptory that Brothers Alexander St. Clair and Eric Smythe have arrived from Madrid."

The sergeant saluted silently and rode ahead. He knocked on the door to the Commandery and received an answer. The sergeant who had gate duty sent a runner to the Preceptor of Champagne and Commander of the Paris Preceptory, Brother Ian McAndrews, a Scottish Templar who Alexander had actually met when he was Earl of Roslin. Ian had been assigned to the Edinburgh Commandery under the command of Robert de Burghe.

When the two Templar knights, and their retainers, rode through the gate, Brother Ian's sergeants rushed out to take horses. The soaked Templar knights were led into the foyer of the Paris Preceptory (more popularly known as the Paris Temple), where they were greeted warmly and supplied with soft linen towels to wipe away the rainwater. They were led directly to a large room, equipped with only two beds, where they removed their chain mail and handed it over to a sergeant who would take it for drying to prevent rust. They then put on dry robes and made their way back to the front hall, where they were led into the great hall.

Brother Ian McAndrews sat on a similar throne to that recognized as Brother Thibauld's back in Madrid and both men bowed low, a gesture waved off by Ian. His Scottish burr was quite thick. "Nonsense, my Brothers, it is I who should be bowing to such brave defenders of the Faith. Welcome to Paris." He braced both men's arms and led them away to a small dining hall. The table they found was quite substantial and they were welcomed to feast to their heart's content.

"Brother Geoffrey will not be arriving for a couple of days and I know you will wish to rest up before his arrival. This terrible weather has really slowed things down."

Neither of the new arrivals spoke much as they ate. They were content to let Ian talk himself out. Alexander's head came up at the next statement, though.

"By the way, Brother Alexander, Worshipful Brothers Michael O'Brian and Robert de Burghe send their warmest greetings and wishes for your health and safety."

This piqued Alexander's curiosity. "Tell me, Brother Ian, do you have a way I might send them each a letter?"

"But, of course. My secretary can supply you with writing materials. If you wish, he can also take dictation."

Alexander's eyes had gone distant in remembrance. "No, that is all right. I would rather write myself."

Ian was pleased with his reaction. Most Scottish knights he had known could read and write, even as much of the non-British nobility was illiterate. It was a small conceit that Ian held, as rumor had it that even Jacques de Molay himself was unable to read and write. Still, it was a conceit the Scot held dear.

Small talk continued for the better part of an hour before the pair of new arrivals sought their respective beds. The two men, as long compatriots as most in the Temple could even remember, stripped out of their robes and doused all of the lights save one. Both men were long practiced in ignoring the light of one burning candle as they sought sleep.

It was three days later before Brother Geoffrey de Charney, Preceptor of Normandy, rode into the Paris Temple. The summer storms had held them up more than they had expected. But it was bright and sunny when Charney and his crew settled from their saddles and were led in to meet with Brother Ian and the others.

He was greeted with the pomp and ceremony due to one of his rank and Alexander took the opportunity to study him. Geoffrey was not a physically-imposing man. In fact, he was rather short. His eyes, however, told the real story. There was a blazing intensity there, a spirit that was as indomitable as the will of God Himself. He seemed made of an iron spring, coiled to attack at a moment's notice. Alexander believed his reputation for quick action and absolute valor was probably well earned. When it came time, Alexander accepted the ritual embrace from Geoffrey. The two men's eyes briefly locked and Geoffrey nodded slightly, as familiar with Alexander's story as Alexander was with his.

After a sumptuous feast and afternoon prayers, Alexander was ordered to a conference with the Preceptor of Normandy. Brothers Ian and Eric were also in attendance there.

Geoffrey was cool as he looked over all three men. "Most Worshipful Grand Master Jacques de Molay has commissioned the three of you to undertake a unique duty, of special importance to the Order. In fact, it will be of the utmost importance to the Order."

Eric spoke into the silence left as Geoffrey paused. "How important, exactly?"

Geoffrey grinned coldly at the young Englishman. "Why, Brother Eric, the mission you will undertake is to assure the survival of the Order of the Temple, at any cost."

What Eric, whose office was really rather junior, was not aware of was the feud arising between Grand Master Jacques de Molay and Philip IV, the King of France. Both of the older Templars were aware of it, but neither knew its real severity.

Philip was hurting for funds, his treasury depleted by expensive wars and elaborate courts, which were not being covered by adequate taxation. This meant that Philip had to get money from somewhere. He approached the Grand Treasurer of the Order, a French knight named Hughes de Pairaud, for a loan. Hughes forwarded the request on to Jacques de Molay with his recommendation to approve the loan. Molay, however, had no love for the French monarch and denied the loan, seeing it as a serious risk, as Philip already had a great number of outstanding debts.

This obviously angered Philip, who hit upon a possibility to gain control of the Temple. He suggested a new crusade under a new military order, combining the Temple and the Knights Hospitaller of St. John under one command, a warrior king that would be hereditary rather than elected, as Templar and Hospitaller Grand Masters were. And, of course, King Philip offered to be the warrior king in question. This was a laughable proposal to say the least, and obviously one offered to further the power of Philip. No Pope would ever grant such an obvious request, favoring the King of France over other powerful Catholic kingdoms.

That is, until the papal election of 1305, after the death of Benedict XI, when Cardinal Bernard de Got, then-Archbishop of Bordeaux, was elected to the Papacy and took the name Clement V. Clement was an acknowledged friend of France, having already started discussions to move the Papacy from Rome to Avignon, thus strengthening France. Many felt that if he was willing to grant Philip this great concession, merging the two great military orders would be a very small thing. This belief caused a great deal of consternation among the members of the Temple.

Thus, they had been called to this meeting with the Preceptor of Normandy, a Templar who all knew was well-acquainted with the intrigues and intricacies of European royal politics, and who had the ear, and the trust, of the Grand Master of the Order himself.

"Most Worshipful has learned of a plot laid on against the Order, to extort the wealth of the Temple or destroy it. His Majesty King Philip has commissioned his sheriffs and bailiffs throughout France to arrest all the Templars in France in late October or early November. He has already trained them for this, with a mission last year. In a day, all of the Jews in France were rounded up, their property seized, and they were expelled from the kingdom. This will not, however, both Most Worshipful and I are sure, be a case of expelling the Templars from France, but imprisoning us, perhaps even executing us, on charges of heresy.

"This, with His Holiness' support, will no doubt lead to the suppression, if not outright dissolution, of the Order. We will have to go underground if we are to survive.

We will have to subdue our desire to be perfect, holy knights and join with the families of a nation to maintain our survival. That is why the three of you were among those chosen.

"You are all British. Two of you are Scottish and Most Worshipful believes, and I agree with him, that the ripest of kingdoms for this mission is Scotland. As we speak, Robert the Bruce, who was crowned King of Scotland last year, wages a guerrilla campaign against King Edward Longshanks, who is marching north to renew combat against him. Through contacts in Scotland, we believe that you three and perhaps four or five others can infiltrate the royal families of Scotland and help to build a kingdom where our Order can be preserved."

Silence reigned as the three British knights looked at each other and at the Preceptor of Normandy. None of them really knew what to say. Ian was the first to come to his senses. "What about the leadership? Will you and Most Worshipful be going with us?"

Geoffrey shook his head. "No. We, along with most of the recognized leadership will be staying behind. If Most Worshipful disappeared, there would have to be a search. If a few of our less-known figures disappeared, it's easy to write it off."

Alexander's mind went to operational matters. "When and how will we escape King Philip?"

"Our fleet is in port at La Rochelle. When our spies inform us that capture is imminent, we'll order the flight of the fleet. We'll also send a great deal of gold and other treasures that will help to finance the escape and our support for the Bruce."

Eric had still not said anything. Alexander turned to him. "Your thoughts, Brother Eric?"

The English Templar just swallowed hard and shook his head. "I'm just a simple cavalryman, my Brother. I wonder if I'm qualified for this."

Alexander nodded and turned his attention back to Geoffrey. "He makes a good point about qualifications. All the Brothers who escape to Scotland will have to lead. That is a job for Masters. Brother Eric is only a Fellow."

Eric's confusion was almost comical. Geoffrey's smile was genuine. "Is that a nomination, Brother Alexander?"

The Scot nodded. "Yes."

Brother Ian joined the conversation. "I concur, Brother Preceptor."

"Then, so ordered. We will raise him tonight." He turned to the still-confused English knight. "Congratulations, my Brother. Tonight you will receive finally all the hospitality this house can offer."

Chapter 23

Most Worshipful Jacques de Molay, Grand Master of the Temple, was escorted into the main hall of the Paris Preceptory. Ian McAndrews had given up his customary seat to Brother Pierre de Louge, Master of the Temple in France. Brother Ian sat to his right and to Brother Pierre's left sat Brother Hughes de Pairaud, Grand Treasurer of the Order.

The Most Worshipful was escorted by Brother Geoffrey de Charney and Brother Geoffrey de Gonneville, the Preceptor of Aquitaine. Where Charney was short and squarely built, with powerful shoulders and a broad gait, Gonneville was tall and lanky, his thin form looking light enough to be blown away by the first stiff breeze.

However, Alexander was taken aback at the grandeur of the figure of Jacques de Molay. The Grand Master was tall and solidly-built, like a stout tree. His shoulders, even in his sixties, displayed inherent physical strength that few men could hope to match. His back was straight and his stride long. A closely-cut ring of white hair surrounded a spot that had gone bald with age and his face was weathered and deeply lined. His beard was luxurious and hung down to his chest. His white tunic was immaculate, a red papal cross decorating the chest. A similar cross in gold hung from a purple collar around his neck and a white robe was wrapped around his shoulders with a matching red cross on the left side of his chest. Gold and purple thread decorated his sword belt.

The three on the eastern thrones stood and stepped to floor level. All three men kneeled in front of the Grand Master of the Order. The other Templars followed their lead, lowering themselves to their left knee as they would to a sovereign lord. A deep bow was given in return by Molay. At this, the assembled rose to their feet. Brothers Jacques and Pierre exchanged a ritual embrace and Pierre led the Grand Master to the thrones on the eastern dais. Molay took the center chair, seating himself in a manner that could only be described as regal. Pierre sat to his right and Ian to his left, with Hughes on his own left.

Settling himself into the chair, Molay waved to the assembly. "Be seated, my Brothers." There was a general rustling as all returned to their seats. Alexander turned his attention back to the dais to find Ian standing and facing the Grand Master.

"Most Worshipful," he began, bowing low, "allow me to welcome you back to this, your home Preceptory, on behalf of your brother knights of Paris."

The Grand Master returned a slight smile and a nod. "I thank you, Brother Preceptor and Commander, for the hospitality of this, my first house."

There was general applause for the Grand Master.

Alexander sat through the rest of the presentations to the Grand Master, only half-listening. He found his mind wandering more lately than it ever had before. The former Earl of Roslin chuckled silently to himself. Perhaps it was a sign of advancing age.

The interminable presentations on behalf of the several groups of the Temple finally ended, and a general milling-about began as the Templars began making their way to lunch.

Alexander sat in the cool afternoon air, polishing the mail of his armor. While his hands worked at the job, his mind drifted, remembering family and friends long gone, some forever. His parents' faces came unbidden to his mind, Edward and Irina would doubtless be proud of their son. Adolph von Trieste and his legacy of one last charge against a Moorish foe. Brian Kennedy, bleeding the ground red at Stirling defending the back of his friend, compatriot, and noble lord. Fiona, the woman he only wanted to spend eternity with, gone in childbirth. Other faces appeared in his mind's eye, some recent, others far in the past. He stopped polishing long enough to wipe a single tear from his eye.

A shadow passed over him and he looked up. The sergeant was an Entrant still, too young yet to be sent off to fight in the Iberian or German kingdoms. He had the look of awe in his eyes. "Beg pardon, Brother Knight?" His accent was thick with France.

Alexander nodded, remembering the youth's name. "Yes, Brother Guy."

Guy swallowed hard. "Most Worshipful desires to meet with you at your earliest convenience."

Alexander looked down, hiding a grin in his beard. "At your earliest convenience" was no doubt merely a polite way of saying "right away". He set the mail to his side and glanced over at his own sergeant, an Italian. "Brother Guido, please finish this for me." He still saw no reason to lord his position over anyone.

"Yes, Brother Alexander." Guido nodded his acquiescence. Alexander followed Guy off.

Arriving at the chambers that had been granted to Jacques de Molay, Guy saluted and strode away, allowing Alexander to knock on the door of the Grand Master.

The voice was gruff from within. "Come."

Alexander opened the door and strode in. He dropped to his left knee as Molay looked up from a document. The Grand Master grunted. "Get up, my Brother. There is no need for such things in private before an old man." Alexander stood and was waved to a seat. Molay used a glass to read the document before him. This was a shock to Alexander, who had always been under the impression that Most Worshipful was illiterate.

The older man grinned and tapped the glass as he set it down. "It's a well-cultivated lie, and one which comes in handy when I want to pretend not to be too smart in front of such great men as His Holiness Clement or His Majesty Philip. It's quite liberating not to have to read their documents because they think I can't." The two Templars chuckled at that. The Grand Master poured two glasses of wine and both men sipped at it.

"It's a bold grape, Brother Alexander, don't you think?"

Alexander nodded. "Yes, Most Worshipful."

Molay sighed, a small smile on his face. "Do me one favor, if you will. I am so often called 'Most Worshipful' that I wonder if anyone remembers my name. One Master to another, please make it 'Brother Jacques'."

Alexander found this most endearing in a man who had spent so long in such a high office. "As you will, my Brother."

Molay smiled broadly, pleased at the feeling of being treated simply as a Brother. His smile slowly faded as he tossed back the rest of the wine and his eyes hardened. The message to Alexander was clear. It was time to talk about the mission.

"Brother Alexander, I know you have been briefed by Brother Geoffrey on your mission to Scotland. I need you to know, and the others who will go with you, that I expect this to occur very soon, sooner than we have planned for. I feel that the plan to capture us has been sped up by the fact that I must go to Avignon next week. I also feel that shortly after I meet with His Holiness, it will be time to send you away." Jacques looked away, at a calendar.

"It is now October 6, Friday. Tomorrow, after breaking our fast, Brother Geoffrey de Charney and I will leave for Avignon. We will return on Tuesday of next week. Upon our return, you and the others will depart for La Rochelle. Upon your arrival there, the fleet will sail for Dublin. There you will meet with your old mentor, Brother Michael O'Brian.

"Michael pleaded with me not to be given that task, to be allowed to come to France to suffer with us. I could not grant his requests. He will be fully relieved of his vows to return to his position as Lord of Kincora after he sends you to Scotland. His years of loyalty to the Order have meant that much to me.

"In Scotland, you will be led by a Brother Knight to Roslin, where you will find the Master in England and Scotland, another of your former comrades, Robert de Burghe, the only of your band who will not be of one of the islands of Britain. He will lead you in what you must do to disappear into Scottish royal society. He reports to me that he has already discussed these issues with His Majesty Robert the Bruce, who he supported at his coronation two years ago. Brother Robert will continue to serve as Master in Scotland and England and will gain control of Ireland upon your arrival. He has made a request that you be assigned to a dual role as his Seneschal and Marshal. I have granted this request."

Alexander took a second to absorb all of this. His eyes found the older Templar's. "I thank you, Brother Jacques. I hope I will be worthy of this trust."

Jacques smiled warmly. He had known of Alexander's strength and now saw it in the younger man's eyes. "Of course you will, Alexander. Now go, and let me prepare for my journey on the morrow."

Alexander stood and bowed deeply. Jacques picked up the glass again and returned to his reading.

The message had come that the Grand Master would soon be returning. It was clear that it was urgent that they be prepared for departure as soon as he arrived. Seven knights waited for the departure, assisted by one sergeant each. Brothers Ian McAndrews and Eric Smythe waited with Alexander. Alexander nodded to them both and stepped into the building where the other five waited.

Brother John of Sherwood was an Englishman from the heart of the nation. It was well-known to many that he was also an Englishman who had no love for the King of his country. The bluff Templar knight had a chest like a barrel and a midsection that, like a "v", narrowed into a thin waist and hips. All eight of these Templars had been forbidden from cutting their hair for the last four weeks, and Brother John's had grown in thick and a dark reddish-brown. He had scraped off his beard but left a mustache that drooped down to his chin.

The other English Templar was Brother Kenneth Taggart. The combat veteran from the Madrid Temple had been aware of his family connection with Brother

Alexander since the former had become Marshal of Castile and held his deceased Cousin Edward with more than a little contempt. He was the younger son of Edward St. Clair's first cousin and had never really fit in with his family's friends. In fact, he had rather admired William Wallace and the stories that came down from the north. He was more than a little pleased to be going with Alexander to Scotland.

Patrick McStevens and Malcolm O'Shaughnessy made up the Irish contingent. Both known to Brother Michael in Dublin even from before his Templar days, they were proud to be carrying the standard of the Temple, even into obscurity.

Peter Stuart was of Scottish blood, even though his travels had never taken him to Edinburgh. Stuart was the only personally unknown quantity of the group to Alexander, but came with a rich record of service from the Temple in Berlin, where he had served with distinction in combat against the remnants of pagan Germanic society, a task more often done by the Teutonic Knights.

The men all looked up as Alexander cleared his throat. "Most Worshipful will be here soon. Be prepared to depart upon his arrival."

Nods answered his statement and the men returned to caring for their equipment. Alexander glanced over his own baggage, seeing all in order, and returned to the courtyard of the Paris Temple.

He was there when the gates opened and Grand Master Jacques de Molay appeared, attended by a long caravan of mounted Templar knights. The senior Chaplain in France rode to his right, the sun glinting off the gold cord set into rich green Templar robes. The stark white of the Grand Master's uniform positively gleamed in the bright noon sun.

A sergeant took the reins from Molay as he dismounted. He crossed quickly to speak to Alexander. "My Brother," he began, "word is that tomorrow's the day. You and your band must ride immediately for La Rochelle."

"At your command, Grand Master." Alexander sketched a salute and returned to the barn, where the other knights were already mounting, tipped off by the Grand Master's decisive movements.

Alexander pulled himself onto his own steed and turned to address the others. "We ride for La Rochelle," he ordered, leading away with his horse.

The others turned and followed.

Chapter 24

Jacques de Molay sat across from Geoffrey de Charney at a table in his private quarters. The two old warriors shared a companionable silence as the world fell in around them.

Word had come from his agents at La Rochelle. The bailiffs of King Philip IV Plantagenet, ruler of the Franks, had come up empty when they appeared at dawn. The fleet had sailed for several ports shortly before, one of them carrying the bulk of the treasure and eight Templar brothers to Scotland. He smiled at that. He had been worried that they'd waited too long to send those men away. But the gamble had paid off.

Molay stretched his hand out and grasped the mug of red wine, taking a long sip, as the sounds of cracking wood rang in his ears. He knew it signaled the arrival of Philip's troops at the gates of the Temple. He had ordered that no Templar should resist. Their numbers had already been shrunk at his order. Numerous knights and combat-ready sergeants had been dispatched to the German territories and Iberian peninsula, places where their worth as fighting men would overrule any doubts as to their personal proclivities.

He knew what they would be accused of. Charges of heresy, idolatry, usury, and homosexuality would merely be the tip of the iceberg. He knew also that there was no defense from them, that they would begin their trials as guilty men and that torture was the means that Philip's men would use to prove the charges. He knew that he would be tortured personally in private, that he would have to endure pain again before he could confess, lest the torturers think he lied about his own guilt. He knew that he would have to confess to the charges, so that his Order could disappear, for his guilt would wipe away the hunters from chasing down more of his brethren. He feared his name would be cursed for eternity on this level of existence, even as he believed that Christ would forgive his lies in pursuit of extending the service of the Temple on Earth. He said a silent prayer, entreating God directly, to spare his men from as much pain as possible. He had instructed his chief officers in what they must do, how they must endure, and that they would spend their remaining years in prison, accused of crimes they did not, could not, commit. He prayed further that God would shorten all of their lives so that they would not suffer for too long.

The heavy banging was now at his door. He locked his eyes on Charney's and knew that Geoffrey would never betray the secrets, the orders, that he had been given. The fleet was safely away. The corner of the Preceptor of Normandy's mouth turned up and Molay could almost see the thoughts echoing in his brain, the dream of Templar sailors making their way up and down the coasts of Europe, Africa, and Britain, the Templar ensign flying bravely, the black flag with the white skull-and-crossbones becoming even more respected, even feared.

The two men didn't move as the door came down and a half-dozen bailiffs stumbled over each other to get to them. The six stopped short at the lack of a response. For a moment, silence reigned in the room. It was broken by the entrance of Sir Guy, the Sheriff of Paris. Guy was a hulking man with a thick, drooping mustache and a patch over a long-lost left eye, an eye that had been taken when he had attacked a Templar. Sir

Guy's hatred had grown from that incident, some said from the fact that he had been left alive to suffer indignity from his half-blindness.

The look on his face was one of disbelief. "Well, seize them, you bastards!"

They were yanked up by their arms and pulled to face the Sheriff. He chuckled. "Well, well, if it isn't the Most Worshipful Grand Bastard."

His derisive laughter inspired just the wrong kind of reaction from Molay.

Jacques never made a conscious decision. In fact, the sound of the slap across Guy's face came as something of a shock to the Grand Master. He lost sight of the Sheriff as four men pulled him to the ground, heavy fists raining down on him. He tasted blood as he was pulled to his feet. Sir Guy's hand struck him in a backhand motion. The men restraining Geoffrey struggled to hold him back.

Jacques leveled his eyes at the Sheriff, straightening to his full height and spat one tooth onto the ground at Sir Guy's feet.

With a dismissive gesture from the Sheriff, Molay and Charney were led away.

Alexander St. Clair stood at the bow of the ship, silently re-reading the letter, no doubt a similar tome to that delivered by him to the various captains of the Templar fleet. He turned at the sounds of his fellows coming up on deck.

They were striving to be the paragons of knighthood they were supposed to be, but not one of them had grown up on the sea. Of course, neither had Alexander, but he did have a feel for it. He sighed.

"Brethren, you are all aware of the importance of our mission. If our Grand Master was correct, yesterday, he and all of our fellows in France were taken prisoner. There is reason to believe that, if this is true, there are still Templars free in England, Ireland, and Scotland.

"Unless we receive further direction from the Master in Ireland, we have the following orders in hand, in the form of this letter, given to me from Most Worshipful:

"'My Brothers of the Temple, please know that my gratitude exceeds any emotion I have ever felt before. That gratitude is only closely-matched by the dread I feel for the future of our Order.

"'The furthering of our cause is to be your chief concern. No matter what news you may have of the disposition of your brethren on the continent, you are not to return in your role as Knights of the Temple. You are to remain so far as possible in Scotland, with your only travels being to those places where you may safely go and then only in the guises you will adopt under the leadership of His Majesty, King Robert the Bruce.

"'You are hereby released from your vows of poverty and chastity. In point of fact, I order you to gain wealth and father children in marriage, that the wisdom and good effects of the Order may continue into the future.

"'Remember your vow of obedience. The structure of the Order will continue, though it will be hidden. You always will remain Poor Fellow-Soldiers of Christ and your allegiance to the Temple of Solomon will forever mark your consequence among men and knights.

"'May Christ go with you.'"

The men looked at each other in silence.

Alexander cleared his throat. "The captain informs me that we will arrive in Dublin by midday. Worshipful Brother Michael O'Brian will meet us with a baggage train. He has orders as to the disposition of the wealth. We and the majority of the treasure will proceed to Edinburgh. The rest of the treasure will remain there. Dress yourselves as secular men."

They nodded, still a little dazed, as all they knew receded into the mists of time.

Lord Michael O'Brian, titular Master of the Temple in Ireland and Prince of Thomond, sat atop a huge charger, his flag-bearer carrying the standard of three lions on a field of red that had come down through his family since his ancestor was High King of Ireland. The only mark of his service were his gold-laced belt and gold-hilted sword.

The galley flew a flag of Cypriot service. Its sailors were men dressed and bearded as good sailors, indistinguishable in appearance and dress from the other dozens of sailors in the port at Dublin. It was only their keener eyes and straighter backs that marked the difference that strict military training provided. He knew they were Templars.

The seven men who came off the ship, accompanied by a dozen more, were similarly marked by their style of movement and bearing. One left the band and came up to him. Michael dismounted.

The face he saw was shadowed by recently-shorn beard and was older, but still recognizable as the youth he had known. Michael smiled broadly, his cheeks cold without his own beard.

Alexander smiled back and the men embraced briefly, their old friendship still strong despite years apart.

"How are you, pup?" asked the Prince.

Alexander's face lit up. "Not bad, old dog. And you?"

Michael chuckled back at him. "Well."

The two men glanced around, ensuring their privacy amid the throngs on the wharf. Alexander spoke first. "The segment of the treasure you are expecting is in the first hold."

Michael nodded, turning to one of his men. "The first hold. Mind you get all of it."

"Yes, Sire," he replied, turning and gesturing quickly to a half-dozen other men, who proceeded to board the ship.

The old knight and his former squire stood in a companionable silence while Michael's men continued their work.

Chapter 25

Three years had passed since the arrest of the Templars and the nine who had been assigned the task of blending in to Scottish society had done just that. By point of fact, they had become the highest order of society under King Robert the Bruce, who ruled Scotland under a banner of armed truce with the English King Edward II, who was disrespected not only by the Scottish nobility but by his own as well.

Brother Alexander St. Clair, better known as Sir Alexander Sinclair, Duke of Roslin, waited nervously for the arrival of his promised bride. He and the Master were the only two yet to take wives. Alexander had purposely put it off for as long as possible. Even now, he was not sure if he truly wanted to be married. His nerves must be getting the best of him, he realized, as he had just missed what his closest friend and the Master of the Temple in Britain had said.

He gently cleared his throat. "I apologize, Worshipful, but I missed that last bit."

Brother Robert de Burghe, now Sir Robert Burke, Duke of Galway, grinned indulgently. His French accent had all but disappeared and now merely sounded like an affectation appended to a Scottish burr. "I merely asked your opinion of Brother Kenneth's suggestion that, as King Robert has become our great if secret patron, we initiate him into the Order."

Alexander's eyes narrowed. Kenneth had suggested the same thing to him a fortnight before and the two men had argued into the night over it. Kenneth, silver-tongued devil that he had become, had finally won the Seneschal over to his point of view. "Brother Kenneth and I killed many a bottle of good wine over this topic recently. As dawn broke and we took stock of the fallen soldiers around us, I came to agree with him. King Robert should be offered membership in our Order, at least as an associate member."

Robert considered this for several moments, nodding absently. He had also considered the idea of associate membership, a long-held tradition of the Temple that allowed for men of means to enter the Order as supporters. In the olden days, such membership had allowed a man to wear the tunic and robes of a Templar while maintaining his wife and family in the manner they were accustomed to. The idea was that, should he become widowed, a piece of his fortune would go to support his family while the bulk of it became the property of the Order and he became a full member, bound by the same vows of poverty, chastity, and obedience. As his orders had released the Templars of his party from the vows of poverty and chastity, he was unsure how that might affect such membership.

Alexander watched the Master, allowing his brain to come to terms with whatever decision he might reach. "When we convene Chapter next month in Edinburgh, I will ask Brother Kenneth to propose his idea. We will discuss associate membership and what it must mean in our modern times then."

The Seneschal nodded. He knew that Robert's decision was the right one.

Now, he watched the Frenchman's eyes become mischievous. "Now, your bride is to arrive soon, is she not, my old friend?"

A nervous grin crossed the warrior's face. "His Majesty King Robert suggested a match with the House of Stewart. They are the next in strength of claim to the throne and he felt that a union between the Houses of Stewart and Sinclair would strengthen both lines."

Robert chuckled. "And a good Scottish woman to warm your bed won't come amiss."

Alexander's grin deepened. Despite his old friend's lack of a marriage, he was aware that several unattached ladies-in-waiting to the Queen had warmed his bed. It had become a running joke between them that it would take two or three women to satisfy his needs, an interesting statement on the proclivities of a man who had been a monk.

Not that Alexander had maintained his own vow of chastity any better. His clean-shaven face and now-long hair had attracted the attention of many of the prettier ladies of the Scottish court and of several Irishwomen in his holdings across the sea. It was not the prospect of sex but of love that scared the Duke of Roslin.

A knock came from the door. "Come," ordered Sir Alexander.

His own personal seneschal, an Irishman named Anthony Griffith, entered. "Sire, a carriage has just arrived bearing the colors of the House of Stewart. I believe that your intended has arrived."

Alexander nodded. He brushed his tunic and made sure that his kilt was straight, the sporran in its proper location. He nodded to Robert, who followed closely as he made his way to the courtyard.

The carriage stopped short at the end of a welcoming carpet that should keep the feet of the lady clean. Alexander took a deep breath. He knew that Leah Stewart was no virgin, having been married before. He wondered at this woman who had spent the last several years in Ireland and even distantly worried that a crotchety old woman might step out of the carriage, even though he knew that she had only passed twenty-six years. He squared his shoulders as the door opened.

Lady Leah Stewart was a vision in a dress of vivid green. The tartan of the House of Stewart crossed in a sash from her right shoulder to her left hip, unmarked by the tartan of Clan Davidson, even though her now-deceased husband had been a member of that Clan. Her light-brown hair was bound at the back of her head and hung to her waist. Eyes of vivid blue studied every detail of the compound at Roslin, finally coming to rest on its lord. She stepped forward, proud and lengthy strides, to stand before the Duke. She swept her dress out as she curtsied smartly in a motion that would have shamed the grandest dame of the courts at London or Paris.

Even as she did so, her eyes never left Alexander's. They both would know that such an affront was of the gravest seriousness, but Alexander quickly realized that he did not care about being offended in such a simple manner by this woman. She gave off an air of strength and vitality, of confidence and power. Alexander found himself completely infatuated with her and realized that he was becoming more than a little aroused. At once, he was glad for the weight of the sporran that held his kilt, and what it covered, down.

He acknowledge her curtsy with a nod and a half-smile that showed how impressed he was with her imperious manner. He radiated his own brand of strength and confidence and instinctively knew that she would be pleased by them. He knew she would only respect strength and then only if displayed properly.

"My Lady," he said simply.

"My Lord," she replied, her voice resonant and deep, but with an unmistakable femininity.

He extended his arm and she accompanied him to the table, where they would dine and discuss the marriage contract.

Alexander had been quietly pleased at the ease of negotiation. It was as if they simply wanted the same things. Most of all, he knew how attracted he was to her and believed that he had detected a similar attraction from her. He dried his face and looked at himself in the mirror over the basin, studying his own nude form.

He had passed his fortieth year but maintained himself in superb physical condition, brought about by his military training and practice. His shoulders were broad and his arms thick with muscle. He looked down at the play of sinew and muscle in his thighs and calves. The wrinkles around his eyes had cut deep lines that made him look like a predator while the first silver hairs at his temples looked like veins of iron rather than age. He felt that he made a fine physical specimen.

The knock at the door awakened him from his reverie and he hastened to it, covering himself with a silk robe and tying it before opening the door.

A guard stood outside and he could see Lady Leah Stewart behind him. She was clad in a robe as well.

"I'm sorry, my Lord, but she insisted."

Alexander waved a hand to the guard. "It's alright, James. How may I assist you, my Lady?"

"There was a final point to the marriage contract that I must discuss with you immediately, my Lord."

Alexander, puzzled, nodded. "As you wish. I will send for a secretary and Master Griffith. I will meet you in the hall as soon as I dress."

She shook her head. "There's no need for that. I merely need to speak with you in private regarding this manner."

Alexander held himself still, aware of the impropriety of what she suggested. Something in him said to grant her request. "Very well. James, return to your post."

James saluted smartly and returned as Alexander ushered Leah into his chamber. He closed the door behind her and watched her study the room for several moments.

He cleared his throat. "What do we need to discuss, my Lady?"

"Call me Leah," she said softly. He watched as her robe fell from her shoulders and took several seconds to study her from behind. Her back was straight and obviously strong, her shoulders narrowing to a slender waist before flaring out to a magnificent rear end, with perfectly plump buttocks. Her thighs were full and her calves thick. Alexander felt himself start to grow with arousal.

She looked back at him over her shoulder. "Are you going to just stand there, Alexander?" Her tone was more than inviting. And the Duke of Roslin wasted no time in crossing the room to stand behind her, dropping his own robe to the ground as he did so.

His hands went to her hips as he pressed his swollen manhood against the cleft of her butt. His lips found hers and they kissed deeply. Her lips parted and he drove his tongue into her mouth, tasting her fresh breath. His hands slid up to cup her full breasts and his thumbs crossed her nipples, bringing them to a stiffness to match his own.

He stepped back and turned her in his arms. Her breasts stood proudly out from her chest and the small pooch of her stomach sheltered a tangled mass of hair that grew between her legs. He looked back to her eyes and caught her gazing longingly at his thick manhood, fully erect and ready for her.

She stepped forward and kissed him again, their tongues flashing against each other in a dance of desire and passion. Her hand slipped between them and she wrapped a fist around him, stroking him gently and bringing a groan of pleasure from his lips. His arms tightened around her and he lifted her from her feet. A pleased grunt escaped her as he settled her onto the bed and the tip of his throbbing penis brushed the tender moistness of her vagina. She looked confused as he stepped back.

She opened her mouth to speak but Alexander's finger across her lips silenced her. The ease with which he commanded her forced her to respond as he wished. He went to one knee at the foot of the bed, pushing her legs far apart. She gasped at the cool air on her dampness then moaned deeply as his lips touched her. His tongue massaged her labia and she responded with a flare of her hips. He kissed and fondled with his fingers all around her swollen lips and opening. She gasped again as his tongue caressed the opening and moved down to sample the flavor of her perineum and anus. Nobody had ever kissed her as well or as completely as Alexander. She could feel her clitoris throb as the hood pulled back but Alexander declined to kiss it, to fondle it, even to acknowledge it. Her breathing quickened with every touch, every kiss, as his fingers entered her with the familiarity of an old lover. Her hips bucked as his fingers contacted a secret spot in her depths, a spot she didn't know that anyone knew about. Her heart sang when he touched it, but he quickly pulled away. She thought she would go mad with desire as he continued to caress her, to pleasure her, but ignored those things that she knew he must do to give her ultimate pleasure.

Then he stopped. For a second, he froze, not kissing, not massaging, his fingers closed in her depths, his lips and tongue not even touching her. For a heart-breaking moment, she worried that he would never finish what he had started.

His lips and tongue impacted her clitoris with force as he pushed her button inside. She could contain herself no longer, bucking her hips repeatedly against him as wave after wave of sweet pleasure washed over her. She screamed with the intense joy she felt. She almost fainted with it.

When she finally opened her eyes, Alexander was slipping his fingers from her channel and standing at the foot of the bed. Though he had wiped his face, she could see the tracks of her own moisture on his chin as he grinned wickedly at her. She smiled back lazily and looked down at his erection, which bobbed between her legs. She considered for a moment letting him enter her, but knew the possible consequences of that action. Instead, she would just give him what she had come here to give him.

"Your turn," she said.

Alexander nodded as with perfect understanding and backed up a step as she stood. It took a second for her balance to return but she turned him around and laid him on the bed. She stretched out across him, her lips parting as she took him in her mouth. The salty tang of his fluids brushed her tongue and she continued to lower her lips onto him.

She felt his erection brush the back of her throat and slipped it most of the way out. Still, her lips encircled the head and her tongue fondled the very tip. She lowered herself back down on it until it again filled her mouth. Her eyes looked up to see that his were closed as he enjoyed the sensations she gave him.

Leah smiled around his manhood before engulfing it again. She continued, increasing the pace, slowing when he got close to his own climax, knowing that eventually he would go over the hill. And then he did. His hips bucked a little and she sucked him as far in as he would go. She felt his stiffness jerk in her mouth and she could taste the bitter salt of his seminal fluids. She swallowed in reflex before a second spurt fired into her mouth.

She held him in her mouth until he started to soften. She quietly got off the bed and reached for her robe, pulling it on and tying it. She turned to look back at Alexander, surprised by his open eyes.

He moved with the speed and grace of a lion, gliding smoothly to her and roughly pulling her into a deep embrace. She was surprised again as his lips found hers. They kissed deeply and she tasted her own fluids combined with his in an intoxicating mixture.

Their lips parted and he still had that grin on his face. "Sweet dreams, Leah," he said, a chuckle in his voice.

"No doubt they will be now," she said, turning lazily around and redressing in her robe before leaving her Lord's bed chamber.

Chapter 26

Sir John of Sherwood, the Marshal of Britain, let his voice out in a low growl. "I do not believe that to have been the intent of the Grand Master, Worshipful."

Alexander watched as a couple of heads nodded around the room and worried for a moment. He stood slowly, letting the other eight sets of eyes in the room light on him. As he rose in opposition, Sir John looked almost crestfallen. His face maintained a strong bravado, but his eyes looked bleak.

"With all due respect to the Brother Marshal, I must disagree. "Alexander had addressed himself directly to John, but now faced the rest of their Brethren. "Brother Jacques and the rest who formulated this plan could never have imagined the changes our Order would have to make to exist into the future. King Robert has been a bulwark of strength akin to Hiram of Tyre's support to Solomon. To grand him membership in our Order would reward his friendship."

Alexander nodded to the Master before sitting again at his right hand.

Robert Burke let his eyes roam as the Seneschal was seated. He noted a greater number of nodding heads than before. "Has any Brother anything further to offer on this matter?"

Silence enfolded the room and he nodded.

"Then we will vote."

It had been a massive shock to each knight when he had first sat in a meeting of Templar Masters. Everywhere else, the Order was autocratic, but as those who had achieved the rank of Master had proven their ability to lead, it was believed that each man's voice of experience was vital. So, in a meeting of Masters, every man's vote counted. And the voice of the majority ruled.

"All in favor of Brother Ian's proposal to bring new members into the Order again, vote yes by the usual sign." Six right hands rose. "Hands down. Any opposed, vote by the same sign." Two hands rose in opposition. He nodded once. "It passes."

The meeting done and closed, the nine Templars removed the lambskins girded about their waists and resumed their sword belts. There was no rancor about their earlier disagreements. Rather, those who had disagreed with the majority now cheerfully conformed, secure in the knowledge that their Brethren had the Order's best interests at heart.

The conversation among the Templars, now in their roles as Scottish nobles, turned to the next day's festivities regarding the weeding of Sir Alexander Sinclair, Duke of Roslin, to Lady Leah Stewart, still titular Duchess of Orkney. Alexander received much good-natured ribbing from his married companions as they made their way to the dining hall for the noon meal.

As the other eight made their way to lunch, Alexander broke away to attend to his official duty for the Order.

He stopped before the doors of his most sumptuous guest suite and knocked. A burly guard opened the door, bowing deeply when he recognized Alexander. The Duke of Roslin entered and approached Matthew Mornay, Robert the Bruce's private secretary. "Master Mornay," he began stiffly, "see if His Majesty will receive me privately."

Mornay was not privy to the great state secret of the Templar disappearance into Scottish society. So far as he knew, Alexander Sinclair had been a minor noble from the Highlands who had made a major splash to be granted Roslin and his title three years before, a full year before Mornay had been selected by King Robert for his own post.

He also knew that King Robert held the Duke in high regard and hurried into His Majesty's private chamber to announce Roslin's arrival.

Mornay bowed his way out and nodded sharply. "My Lord Roslin, His Majesty will receive you."

Robert the Bruce had changed markedly in the fourteen years since the two had met at Wallace's consecration. The hair that was braided down his back and the beard he sported were flecked with gray and lines had been etched deeply into his face. He still bore obvious physical strength despite the shoulders that slumped and the exhaustion that his eyes betrayed.

Still, those tired eyes sparkled as Alexander entered and the doors were closed behind him. And Alexander was touched by the man's charisma as he waved him over. "Come, old friend. Sit with me." Alexander grinned as he sat on the bench, aware that the younger man had learned much from the legend left by men such as Wallace, Moray, and even St. Clair.

"Tell me, Alexander, what news do you bring from your Brothers of the Temple?"

Alexander, unsurprised by the King's knowledge of his appearance, cleared his throat. "We wish to extend to you the hospitality of the house and in the name of Almighty God, initiate you as a Knight of the Temple."

The Bruce's shoulders straightened as he nodded slowly. "I thank you fro honoring me so."

Alexander responded with his own nod. "You honor us with the help you have rendered to the Order." He shifted on the bench. "As you are no doubt aware, in the past, we received new members in a public ceremony which we shortly followed with a private one open only to Templars. As we are no longer public but private, we will receive you tonight." He stood. "Be prepared to receive one of my Brethren at nones."

Robert the Bruce nodded once, recognizing the formality of the moment. "I will."

And Alexander turned on his heel and strode from the room.

The Bruce still looked a little dazed the next day when he gave the bride away at the wedding of Lord Alexander Sinclair, Duke of Roslin, to Lady Leah Stewart, Duchess of Orkney. The wedding would actually grant Alexander power over both lands and make him one of the greater powers in all of Scotland.

Leah was escorted to Alexander's side, her dress of perfect white, a tradition Alexander had insisted upon, since her virginity had been taken in marriage to her first husband. As she was led to him, his mind saw her as she had been in his bed over the course of the previous weeks. They had enjoyed each other, pleased each other, with illicit kisses and sweet touches, but never the ultimate act. Still, the pure pleasure of it was something Alexander had to force from his mind, lest the recollection be too much for him and he become visibly aroused.

Instead, he thought back to the morning reading of the marriage contract, which had then been consented to by Alexander and King Robert, as a representative duly deputized by the Stewart family. It had actually been difficult not to stare at Leah, who sat across from him at the King's side. He had felt like a lad again, and a part of him was pleased by that. He had forgotten what it was to feel young.

The priest intoned Latin as Alexander and Leah stood before him. They made their vows and chastely kissed. For a moment as their lips touched, Alexander wanted to devour Leah and he was almost surprised, not that he should have been, when he saw in her eyes the same wanton desire that must burn in his. As a string quartet played, Alexander led his bride away from the altar and into the dining hall, where a sumptuous meal was served. Her part of the festivities being over, Leah made a small gesture to her attendants and they rose and departed. Alexander was careful not to imbibe too much of the rich red wine that continued to flow after they left.

With the departure of the women, the jokes and stories that rang through the hall became bawdy and lewd. Toasts were given to the groom's manhood and his warm reception into the marriage-bed. Drunkenness prevailed and even Alexander was a little unsteady as he made his way to his bedchamber.

His brain sobered and his breath caught in a tight throat as he beheld his new bride, who again stood naked, her back to him, at the foot of their bed. For her part, Leah looked back over her shoulder at the big Scot and Alexander felt a powerful thrill at the memories her stance invoked. There was a chuckle in her voice as she said, "I wondered if I was going to have to come get you."

Alexander shook his head, a dazed look in his eyes. The thinking part of his brain complained about the silliness of his reaction, recalling nights with Leah and other women, but he could not help feeling a sense of awe at the beauty of his wife.

Her long, light-brown hair hung freely down her back, brushing the top of those plump buttocks that he knew would perfectly fill his hands. Her thighs were silken and he could already imagine their feel in his grasp. His eyes continued their downward journey, pleasured by the vision of her calves and feet.

Leah turned to face him and the heat multiplied in Alexander's loins. His eyes immediately found her heavy, full breasts before trailing down to the light-brown mass of velvet-soft curls between her legs, hiding the mystery of her womanhood, a mystery that was now his. The hair of her pubis had been clipped back to expose the sweet coral of her nether-lips.

This time, she crossed to him, pushing her body against his as the kiss they had wanted to share at the wedding burst forth with unrestrained passion. Leah felt the moan against her mouth as her hands expertly released his kilt and his plaid pooled around his feet. They parted long enough for his tunic and boots to be tossed aside and embraced again. She squealed as his strong hands squeezed her bottom. The squeal became a gasp as he lifted her off the floor and crossed the room, his bobbing erection tapping insistently against her mons.

He laid her back on the bed and stopped to look at her, hair splayed behind her head in a dizzying array. Her eyes commanded him not to hesitate and he gladly obeyed their order. He climbed atop her, locking his lips onto hers, and finding her tight opening with his erection.

Stars exploded behind her eyes as he pushed his thickness into her, so that she nearly lost consciousness at his joyous invasion. She grasped his hips with her hands and urged him to his ultimate depth with her feet against the backs of his thighs. Her breasts were crushed against his muscular chest as they sought to press their bodies completely into one another. A small part of Alexander's mind marveled that, for only the second time in his life, he truly wished to become one with another human being. Then his mind closed down as he picked up the pace of his thrusts, sensing, feeling her on the journey to pleasure alongside him. Her lips spoke breathlessly into his ear, urging him on, until not even that came from her, just soft grunts of enjoyment.

For his part, Alexander took those grunts for the signs of impending joy that they were and deepened his strokes, at the same time maximizing each one's effect. He knew that his own orgasm was approaching, and wanted to make sure that Leah experienced at least as much pleasure as he did.

Her hands moved up his back and tightened their grip around his shoulders as her eyes flew open and her breath was completely stolen by the orgasm. Her legs squeezed his hips tightly of their own accord as his semen flowed into her, his seed washing into her womb with the hope of new life. She held him deep inside of her body for as long as possible, wanting the experience to last forever, knowing that desire impossible.

Exhaustion overtook the newlyweds and they bundled into each other's arms. As sleep captured Alexander, his mind whispered the name, "Fiona". For the first time years, it was not accompanied by a wave of pain. That scar was healed.

As he fell into deep sleep, he mumbled the name, "Leah", into her hair. She squeezed him in her sleep and he squeezed back, truly happy for the first time in a lifetime.

Chapter 27

The war drums again beat in Scotland and tales of a mighty English army under the direct command of King Edward II spread throughout the countryside.

And all over a battle site from the days of William Wallace. The name "Stirling" echoed through the halls of Edinburgh, Glasgow, London, and York. And, of course, Roslin. It gave Alexander something of a headache, remembering the pains and glories of battle against the English foe.

King Robert the Bruce stood at the head of a large table in Edinburgh, in his own mighty fortress, the other nine Templar Masters around the room. One of the newly-made Fellows of the Temple was the subject of the discussion.

"Damn your brother! He should know better than to try and attack Stirling. Then that deal he made for their surrender. He had to know that no son of Longshanks could sit still and let an English castle fall into Scottish hands. It's no wonder they're gathering at York. By St. John's Day, they'll have fallen on every Scot they can find and nocked their ears for treason." John of Sherwood, nominal commander of any Templar force in Scotland as Marshal, was in fine form.

"Calm down, old friend." Burke's voice tried to sooth the buff Englishman, but to little avail. John quieted but continued to pace.

Alexander felt John's anger. He knew that both Burke and the Bruce himself shared it. Edward the Bruce, the King's brother, had laid siege to Stirling Castle during the Lenten season, able to wring from them a promise that they would surrender if no aid came before the end of summer. King Edward II, no great military leader, had nonetheless ordered an army formed and prepared to march against Edward the Bruce's forces. Now, King Robert had the devil's decision between ignoring the entreaties of his own brother and allowing the English to have him, or forming an army to face what had quickly rebuilt itself into being one of the finest military forces in the world: the English army.

A quiet knock sounded on the door and Alexander peered out. "Yes, James?" he asked of his guard outside the room.

James saluted and extended a scrolled letter to him. "Lord Malcolm Davidson brought this and ordered me to give it to you personally."

Alexander's eyes came up quick at the name of one of the rising stars in the new Templar Order. Lord Malcolm had been one of his personal choices and would probably be the next to be granted the boon of being a Master. Only one other Master had been raised since the suppression of the Order and that was the King himself. Alexander thanked the soldier and closed the door.

"Brethren, Lord Malcolm sent this. He's been in Paris for the last months negotiating with King Philip." Alexander broke the seal on the scroll and translated the Latin into English for the others. "He recently witnessed the death …" He blinked hard, unable to believe the words on the page. "… the death of …" Again, hesitation covered him. "… the death of Grand Master Jacques de Molay."

Total stillness and silence engulfed the room. All nine pairs of eyes, even King Robert who had not known the Grand Master, were locked on the Seneschal of Scotland. He found himself without voice, swimming in midstream with no idea what direction the river of his emotions would take him. His eyes sought out the French Master of Scotland. "Worshipful Master, I don't know what ..."

Burke brought himself up from the depths of the Templars' despair. "Does Brother Davidson give any details?"

Alexander's eyes went back to the missive, locating what he sought. "He does. Apparently, the Most Worshipful was brought out to answer the charges publicly, to confess in front of all. He was accompanied by Charney, Gonneville, and Pairaud. They were called forward to answer the charges and Gonneville and Pairaud acquiesced and were sentenced to life imprisonment. When Brother Jacques stepped forward, Charney was with him. He spoke about truth and justice, then denied the charges. It apparently caused quite an uproar, people shouting about injustice and the greatness of the Order. At sunset, Molay and Charney were taken to an island in the Seine and burned at the stake, by order of King Philip himself."

The ten Templar Masters remained in stunned silence while all considered the information they had just received. "Brother Alexander," began the Master, "do we know of any other Templars in existence?"

Alexander shook his head reflexively. "No, Worshipful. We've heard rumors of Templar bands in the German principalities, in Iberia, even in the Balkan territories, but nothing concrete."

Burke's brain was working now, the shock of the moment passed. "So, all we know about for sure are the ten Masters here."

"Yes, sir," replied the Seneschal, his eyes still on the floor.

"And, so far as we know, then, I am the ranking Templar in Christendom."

Alexander's head jerked up. "Yes, sir."

"Very well. Brother Seneschal, Brother Marshal, and Brethren, I hereby order a Grand Chapter called for one week's time from today, at Roslin."

Heads started to nod as brains came to grips with the new knowledge. John of Sherwood's voice rang true in the hall. "And may God have mercy on the soul of our departed Grand Master."

Brother Eric Smythe stood outside the door, clad in Templar robes, guarding the assembly, a sword in his hand.

Inside, the other nine Templar Masters convened the first Grand Chapter of the Order since 1292, some 22 years before. Nine lots were selected, one being the shortest, and Alexander Sinclair held them out to the others. The Brother who drew the short straw would preside over the election, which would be by secret ballot. He also could not be elected Grand Master. Some men prayed to receive the short straw, others prayed never to have that lot fall on him, harboring the desire to lead the Order. When Robert Burke drew a normal length, he sighed deeply. None of the others realized how little he wanted the station that would shortly be his.

Brother Ian McAndrews drew the short straw. He looked around at the others, who now would look to him for the minutes it would take to elect their new leader. No nominations would be spoken and Brother Ian passed out scraps of paper to each man. Inked quills were dipped and names recorded on each paper. Ian took the other eight and counted them. He looked up at the other men and cleared his throat.

"Brethren, you have elevated Brother Robert Burke to the office of *Magister Templi*, Grand Master of all Knights of the Temple."

All sets of eyes lighted on the newly-elected Grand Master. "I thank you for the honor you grant me, my Brethren. I will continue to serve the Temple as I have all of my adult life."

Burke looked around at the others. "I will appoint Brother Alexander to continue as Seneschal, now of the Order itself, and Brother John as Marshal."

Alexander locked eyes with John and both men nodded.

Robert continued as they agreed. "Does any Brother have anything further to offer for the good of the Temple?"

Brother Ian again spoke. "God bless our Grand Master."

The others, Robert silent among them, answered. "Amen."

Robert's voice was alone as he said, "So mote it be."

Chapter 28

Darkness reigned outside as the twenty Templar knights, clad in lightweight white robes, knelt. Father, and Brother, Seamus MacDougal of the Clan Stewart had pulled the green mantle, hidden for seven years by the orders of Jacques de Molay and Robert Burke, from storage and once again consecrated the host for the Holy Communion of Templar warriors. The ceremony meant everything to the nine veterans, even more than to the other eleven. Those nine had once dedicated their lives to Christ and the Temple, and still lived that dedication in their hearts. They had even foregone shaving and had their stylishly-long hair cut off. If they were to die, they felt, it would be better this way.

Thus, they would be recognized at the Golden Gates of Heaven by their Brethren, even by the Choirs of Angels and the Almighty Himself, as Poor Fellow-Soldiers of Christ and the Temple of Solomon.

As Templars.

Sir Henry Bohun, nephew of the Earl of Hereford and one of King Edward's favorites, sat in the manor just away from the battlefield, the final plans now laid out before him.

Sir Roger Taggert, the Duke of Gloucester, whose younger brother Kenneth had run away to join the Templars, had de facto become recognized as leader of these forces and now turned a dark glare on the effeminate knight.

Bohun was laughing shrilly in response to Roger's latest question. "Cavalry?" His laughter faded in the face of Roger's countenance. "My Lord, these are half-witted, undernourished Scots. They don't have cavalry. At best, they'll have their long pikes to stab at our horses. But armored knights on horseback? I think you overestimate their sophistication."

Taggert sighed deeply in his desperation. "I do not think His Majesty will do well to underestimate it. Unsophisticated they may be, but we are talking about men that have nominally been at war for the last twenty years. Some of the men we will be facing tomorrow stood with Wallace …"

"And they will fall, just as Wallace did to the might of England." Neither man had heard the approach of King Edward II and both turned to face the ruler of their country. Edward was just a little shorter than his father had been, but where his father tended to the muscular and martial, Edward the younger had more flesh on his bones and a far more indulgent face. The whispers had grown to out-and-out rumors regarding the company he kept. Stories about the queen spending her nights in a cold bed while His Majesty shared his with his fellows tore quietly at the natures of military men who lived to see the royal paramour happy.

Both men rose before their king and bowed deeply. Despite the fact that he had given Taggert the boon of command, shared as it was with the Earl of Hereford, he had never hidden his dislike for the man. He nodded an acknowledgement to the two and they rose. Edward found a seat and took it. He waved Roger and Henry back to their seats.

Roger took a deep breath and addressed his sovereign. "Your Majesty, while I have little doubt of our victory on the morrow, I wish to risk as few of our men as possible. Thanks to their own proclivities, we have already lost some to petty squabbles, as we did yesterday."

Henry sniffed. "That damn farmer had no right to lay his hands on the King's men."

Roger's head snapped to the other knight. "They were raping his daughter."

"He's just a damn Scot, worth less even than the Bruce. At least he's noble."

Roger dipped his head and shook it. "Yes, the Bruce is noble. And the farmer paid the price for depriving two men-at-arms of a piece of Scottish ass. And he killed one of ours before his fellows took the farmer's life."

Henry now laughed. "And we burned his farm."

"Yes, and murdered his wife and kidnapped all three of his daughters, who then got used for sport by a whole company. It was sickening."

"They're Scots."

"They're human."

Edward interrupted the freshening argument. "My Lords, please. This bickering over a pointless issue of taking liberties with the conquered will do us no good."

"Majesty," said Roger, "this is more than a pointless issue. It goes straight to the heart of good discipline. Your father never had to deal with such an uncontrolled force as this one."

Edward visibly stiffened. "Are you saying I cannot control my troops, Gloucester?"

Roger immediately backtracked. "Of course not, Majesty. It is your sub-commanders, not you."

Edward's visage did not soften. "We'll deal with our commanders in the morning." He nodded curtly to Gloucester. "You are excused."

Roger actually found himself sweating. Like many who were familiar with the King of England, he was aware of Edward's lack of physical courage. But the man was also very willing to fly off the handle and order his sacking, or even execution. He was, therefore, glad to make his escape.

He made it out of the manor and into his tent.

Alexander Sinclair sat at the foot of the bed he would share with his wife. Leah had brought their son William with her from Roslin. The three-year-old was already starting to fade, having been properly entertained. Leah, sewing while "her men" played, put down her knitting and came across the spacious room to pick up the lad. She took him to the nanny in the corner and kissed her son before handing him off to be put to bed.

When the door closed, Leah's hands went up to the bun of her hair, releasing it from its bondage. The two didn't speak as Alexander stood and crossed to stand behind her. His hands worked at the familiar constraints of her dress. As her hair tumbled freely, her dress fell around her feet.

She turned to be lifted from her feet by the strong arms of her husband.

Their lovemaking was intense with their shared love. They both climaxed at the same moment, their cries mixing into the night. They took their turns cleaning up afterward and Alexander doused the candles in the room, leaving one flickering on a bedside table while Leah curled up in his arms.

She actually gave in to the worry that a wife feels for her beloved husband going into combat. "You will be careful?" she asked softly.

Alexander sighed, his eyes locked into the distance. "As careful as I can be, my dear," he replied as softly.

This caused her to pull away and roll toward him, pinning him with her eyes. "Damn it, Alexander! I don't want your patronization. I want a real assurance that you will take no unnecessary risks in combat. There's more at stake than Robert's ambitions here. You're more important to me than that."

Alexander, deeply touched by her concern, again thanked a caring God for this woman, and he fell even more deeply in love with her at that moment. "I swear to you that I will do all in my power to return to you after the battle. But risks are part of my reality."

Leah's hand came up and swiped away a tear as though she were shooing away a fly. "It's just that I don't want to be a widow twice." Her voice quivered with emotion. "And I don't want to raise our children without a father."

The impact of those words shook Alexander. "Children?"

Now the tears were accompanied by a laugh. "Yes. Children. As in, I'm pregnant again. William will have a little brother or …" She didn't have the breath to get the last words out because of the bear hug that Alexander had pulled her into.

When she pulled back to look her man in the eye, Leah saw her own happiness reflected in the tears of joy he had shed. They kissed deeply, the salt on each other's lips an aphrodisiac. Their legs entangled in each other and Leah seated herself on Alexander's erection, her body gripping him into her depths.

They made love in the light of one guttering candle.

Sir Roger Taggart had a difficult time falling asleep, despite the services of the prostitute in his tent. He left her cold embrace and pulled on pants and boots to tour the cool Scottish night.

He longed to plunge his troops into battle against the Scottish. He knew of the interdict placed on the kingdom of Robert the Bruce and saw the next day as his own personal Crusade. He thought back to the days of the great crusading king, Richard the Lion Heart, and longed to join the long-dead Englishmen he had led into battle against the Saracen hordes. He saw himself in his mind's eye, pinning a Mohammedan to the earth with his lance while a force of white-clad Templars cheered him and slapped him on the back. He felt a surge of happiness at the thought that was far deeper than any he had known in a woman's embrace.

Roger's shoulders sagged as he thought about the loss of the Templar Order. He thought of the past-their-prime Knights of St. John who even now paraded the streets of London and York, unwilling to accompany Edward II into battle against the renegade, excommunicate Scots. He even thought back to the promised territory that would be restored to the House of Taggart with their victory against the Bruce. His lips formed the word, Roslin. It had been promised by King Edward himself.

The hatred for Scotland burned deep in the Duke of Gloucester's guts.

A cry from the manor roused him from his thoughts. His eyes went up to a window where light burned from the background. There was King Edward, bracing himself against the windowsill. He released a gargled cry as someone stood behind him. In the light, Roger recognized the figure of Henry Bohun. Both men were nude.

Roger's burning hatred petered out in a moment of disgust.

Not for the first time came the unbidden thought. If this is a crusade, is England on the right side?

Chapter 29

Alexander came to instant wakefulness at the soft knock on the door. He disentangled himself from Leah's arms, drawing a soft moan of protest from her sleeping lips. He padded barefoot to the door and cracked it open.

Sergeant Michael Davidson stood, in full battle dress, in the anteroom. He bowed deeply. "As your Lordship commanded," he offered softly.

Alexander acknowledged his bow with a nod. "I will be down directly, Sergeant." Another bow and the armed man was gone.

Alexander closed the door quietly and crossed to an uncovered window to use the last of the moon's rays to dress.

He wrapped the proper tartan around his legs, closing it with a pin. An undershirt went on, covered with light chain-mail. A tunic of stark white went on over the mail. He seated himself to pull on leggings and boots. His plaid went over a shoulder and he attached a sword belt around his waist. The belt was black and threaded with the gold of his office. The Brethren had agreed to wear only this proof of their Order and rank. He wrapped a robe of white, the black crenellated cross of his family crest on the back, around his shoulders and lifted his helmet. With every article of clothing he donned, the embers that had burned Jacques de Molay at the stake heated within him.

His hand rasped over a week's stubble, the beginnings of his first real beard since his arrival in Scotland. The embers in his heart had reached conflagration.

He crossed the room to stand next to the bed and leaned down to kiss Leah over the eyebrow ever so gently. When he straightened, the moonlight reflected her opened eyes.

"I love you, Alexander," she whispered.

His smile was full of his own feelings. "And I love you, Leah."

With that, he turned on a heel and strode out of their chamber.

When the door closed behind him, the fire of the Templar Order burned white-hot in his soul.

The dawn found King Robert the Bruce in conference with his top military advisers, namely Lord Alexander Sinclair, Sir Robert Burke, and Sir John of Sherwood. Sergeant Michael Davidson stood a respectful distance away.

"How is their army disposed, Alexander?"

"Chaotically, Majesty. Sergeant Davidson reports that their cavalry seems well-prepared, but they have foot soldiers that seem to know little of martial discipline. I believe that a proper attack from whence they least expect it will drive their infantry into chaos. John?"

"I agree, Brother Alexander. If we position our schiltrons properly, and support them with your 'heavy infantry', a cavalry charge into their flank at the proper moment will send them reeling."

Robert spoke up. "I propose one further change. The commander of Edward's cavalry is Duke Roger Taggart," he nodded to Alexander, "your cousin, and a nephew of your father. He was one of the Templars' biggest supporters and, apparently, has wondered into the right ears at the justice of the English cause. Let's make those doubts as real as possible."

The Bruce shook his head, not understanding, even as Alexander nodded resolutely. "I don't understand."

John of Sherwood's gruff voice cut through his confusion. "He means commit all of our Brethren to the cavalry charge, dressed in their proper regalia."

Now the King nodded. "I see. Give the orders. Go now."

The three Templar commanders turned their horses away from their King and began to ride away.

"Bastard Scottish!" The cry was a shock to all three of the men as they made way from the Bruce.

Sir Henry Bohun had broken from cover and they were too far away to reach the King's side in time. He raised a heavy lance and charged hard at the Bruce. Robert took a dim view of his actions, or so the look on his face said. In fact, it was almost a look of pity. His hand reached behind him on his saddle and disengaged a battle axe. He glanced at the Templars.

That glance gave a silent order. As John and Robert began to rein their horses to counter the Englishman's charge, Alexander's hands went out. "No." His voice was that of command, not request. Both men held their peace as Bohun bore down on the Bruce.

It was impossible that the King could counter the charge from a standing position. His horse was not a charger, merely a travel horse that was not trained in the arts of war. The axe didn't have nearly the reach of the English lance.

There was not way for the Scot to triumph.

And Henry de Bohun knew that, too.

He cried out as he drove his lance forward. His face had less than a second to register shock as his weapon did not impact the Scot.

The Bruce's ill-trained horse had sidestepped the lance and the Bruce himself now stood in the stirrups, bringing a mighty downswing onto Bohun's shoulder.

With a sickening crunch, the blade impacted meat and continued its downward journey through the Englishman. With a dead thud, Bohun's body slid from the saddle and fell to the ground. The Bruce's left hand wiped across his brow and came away stained with Bohun's blood. He turned his eyes to the Templar trio and nodded.

The nod was returned by the Duke of Roslin, who then turned to Davidson, who had been as stunned as the rest of them by Bohun's sudden appearance. "Sergeant."

Davidson turned back to Alexander. "Sir?"

"Form a proper bodyguard for His Majesty that will keep such ruffians away from him and prevent him from such foolish activities as trying to get personally involved in this combat any further from what he has done thus far."

The Sergeant saluted. "Aye, sire."

Sir John of Sherwood overlooked the battlefield. He had orders not to accompany his Brethren, but to command the schiltrons and infantry. He chafed a bit at it, but it was a proper order from the Grand Master himself. Both Robert and Alexander had looked saddened at the order's necessity.

The English and Scottish forces had skirmished across a whole day and were now lined up to face each other. The English infantry had had no luck against those schiltrons, especially supported as they were by axe-wielding infantrymen. Sergeant Michael Davidson had proven himself in battle once again before taking a lucky arrow that had been destined for him. Sherwood looked over at the fallen body of Alexander's infantry commander and shook his head. His second, coincidentally from Sherwood's own private force, had also acquitted himself well and had not had the bad luck of his name on an arrow shaft. Sherwood checked the sun and the English disposition, looking for the proper alignments.

Then he saw it. The cavalry came forward, led personally by the Duke of Gloucester. He turned to a runner. "Tell Lord Alexander that Gloucester's leading the cavalry into the center."

"Now we will see if the plan is sufficiently worth leaving our flanks unguarded by cavalry." The King of Scots' voice was full of doubt.

"It's worked before." John of Sherwood's voice was designed to erase those doubts.

Real curiosity appeared in the Bruce's question. "Where?"

Sherwood grinned. "The Muslims of Cordoba were properly respectful of the Temple and believed they were fighting a purely secular force. Brother Alexander personally led the charge into their flank and scattered them to the winds."

Now the Bruce looked confident. "May the Duke of Gloucester be as scared of a ghost as the Muslims of Cordoba were by the Templar cavalry."

"Amen," said John of Sherwood.

"So mote it be," replied Robert the Bruce.

Sir Roger Taggart looked down the marching line of his cavalry. He ordered his men forward at the charge and they obeyed.

The Duke of Gloucester was proud of the battle-roar that his men released at the prospect of slaughtering the Scots.

Then he was dismayed as that battle-roar turned into a questioning sound, then a scream as men were cut down.

He reined in and looked down the line, his eyes questioning. He tried to rub his eyes through his helm, defeated by the metal, but still not believing.

They were clad in white, red crosses splayed on their left breasts. They attacked like madmen, like the berserkers he had heard about from the days of the Angles and Jutes. Their swords rose and fell in unceasing carnage. They didn't slow as the blood of the English cavalry sprayed onto their white tunics and robes, decorating them with the gore of a losing force. Their leader shouted "Beauseant!" as his sword cut through another Englishman.

They were Templars.

And in that moment, Duke Roger Taggart saw his death, possibly his damnation. For the Templars, despite all that French Pope had said, were warriors for God.

And if God was for Scotland, the English were against God.

He knew there was only one way out of this. There was only one way to honor the Almighty in this. The Viking blood that shared his veins with the Norman told him the way. He targeted the commander, whose green eyes had turned away from him. He aimed his lance at the Templar's unprotected back.

He charged.

His aim was thrown off as another Templar flew through the air at him. He had launched himself from horseback at the English commander. The impact drove him from his own mount, forced the lance from his hand. But Taggart was a cunning warrior. Even as they fell, he pulled a dagger from his belt and sank it through tunic and mail into the middle of the Templar.

Roger felt the weight on top of him and heard the death rattle of his breath as his blade cut apart heart, lungs, arteries and veins. He shoved the body of the dead Templar from him and stood, pulling his sword as he did.

The scream of the Templar had drawn the attention of the commander, who wheeled his horse, those green eyes now darkened with hatred and pain. He pulled his horse's rein, causing it to caracole. One heavy hoof struck out at his wrist. He felt the bones break from the force and dropped his sword. He raised the dagger, but was no match for the mounted knight. A flash of steel and Roger Taggart's head rolled from his neck.

He was sure he heard laughter as he died and wondered if it was from angels or demons.

Twenty white-clad Templar knights accompanied the body of Grand Master Robert Burke into the chapel by candlelight. John of Sherwood commanded the detail. Seamus MacDougal intoned the Latin prayers over the fallen knight.

As darkness reigned outside, the Templars, chief among them the victorious King Robert the Bruce, paid the last measures of respect to a fallen Brother, the only one of their number who had fallen in combat. That afternoon, at the insistence of the Brethren, had convened a Chapter. The election was a fait accompli. Unanimously, the Brethren had chosen Alexander to be the Grand Master of the Order of the Temple. He had asked John of Sherwood to remain in his position as Marshal and the gruff English Templar had agreed. He had further appointed Kenneth Taggart, whose brother Roger had fallen under Alexander's sword, to serve as Seneschal. He, too, had consented.

These thoughts rang around Alexander's head as the ceremony proceeded.

Then, it was his turn to step forward. He bent low over the body, praying silently for strength, for courage, for all those things his Brethren believed he never had to ask for.

He straightened and turned to the assembled. It took him a moment to get the word out, but when it came, it came strong.

"Beauseant!"

Epilogue

Glad hands slapped Sir, and now Brother, William Sinclair on the back. He looked around the room at the men he shared brotherhood with.

His father, now he knew to be Grand Master, Alexander Sinclair looked like the proud father he was. William wondered how long his younger brothers would have to wait for this boon. Robert was only fourteen and Michael was only ten. He wondered if they would be made Entrants at seventeen or if their father would hold off on their advancement.

His eyes fell on Kenneth Taggart. The English knight had been a close friend of his father for decades and now William realized why he was considered to be the Duke of Roslin's right hand man in political and military matters. Learning that the Duke of Elderslie was Seneschal of the Order made that make sense.

He looked over at the two older men who sat off to the side. Sir John, the Lord Mayor of Edinburgh, and King Robert the Bruce had retired from active service with the Order as he understood it from the words during the ceremony and the meeting afterward. Still, their council was well-received in all manners regarding the Order of the Temple.

He saw the King separate from the crowd, taking his father with him. After a short discussion, Alexander's eyes traversed the room, settling on the lad. His arm came up in a beckoning motion. He excused himself from discussion with Brother Eric Smythe and crossed the room to their sides.

"Brother William," began the King by way of preamble, "though your father denies it, I am shortly to die. I would like to send you on a quest when that event occurs."

William looked from the King to his father and back. Alexander looked distrustful, but nodded mutely.

"If I can accomplish it, Your Majesty, I will."

The Bruce shook his head sharply. "No, not as a knight of the realm. I do not give you a command; I ask you a favor as a Brother."

The weight of his vows rested on his shoulders as he considered the Bruce's words. He finally nodded resolutely. "As a Brother, I will grant your request."

The King of Scots chuckled softly. "Good. Here is the request. I always swore that I would go on Crusade, but never accomplished the feat."

"I disagree," interrupted Alexander. "We were on a crusade to free Scotland from Edward II."

"You interrupt your King?" The Bruce looked horrified.

Alexander's eyes glittered. "No, Brother Robert, I correct a Templar as his Grand Master."

Before the words finished from his mouth, Robert was already grinning.

"Well, regardless, Most Worshipful, I was asking this Brother a favor."

Alexander nodded, slightly exasperated. "Proceed, my Brother."

"Thank you." He nodded to Alexander and turned his attention back to William. "As I was saying, I never reached Jerusalem to return it to the fold of Christendom. So, I ask that, after my death, you take my heart and bury it as near the Temple Mount as possible."

William nodded. "I will do my best."

Now both men looked at William with grave eyes. "No, Brother William," came Alexander's voice, now not the voice of a father but of a Templar commander, "if you are making this promise, you must swear."

William again felt the weight of his vows as he bowed his head in contemplation. When his eyes came up again, Alexander saw himself reflected in the younger man's gaze. "Before God and my Brethren, I swear it will be done."

William was surprised to see tears of pride in his father's eyes. But they were gone with an eye blink. "Good, Brother William. Very good."

Made in United States
Orlando, FL
26 March 2022